The Old Man and His Dog

The Old Man and His Dog

by
W.G. Vandehulst

Illustrated by
W.G. Vandehulst, Jr.

PAIDEIA PRESS
St. Catharines, Ontario, Canada

First published in Dutch as *Thijs en Thor*, © G.F. Callenbach
B.V., Nijkerk. Translated by Johannes De Viet.

Copyright 1979 by J.H. Enterprises Ltd. © All rights re-
served. Published by Paideia/Premier, P.O. Box 1450,
St. Catharines, Ontario, Canada L2R 7J8. No part of this
publication may be reproduced, stored in a retrieval system,
or transmitted in any form without the written permission
of the publisher.

ISBN 0-88815-767-3
Printed in the United States of America.

Table of Contents

1. To Blue Gate Farm

"Come on, old girl, let's be off! Giddy-up!"

Jamie started off. Her broad paws with their worn-down nails clawed the pavement, and she threw her chest into the harness. With a jerk the two-wheeled milk cart moved ahead. The barrels were on the cart and Jake was behind it. "Giddy-up!"

It was still very early in the morning. It was really still nighttime. The dark streets of the town were empty and silent. Here and there a street light flickered in the wind.

Jamie was in a good mood. She pulled and she barked. Her hoarse voice sounded hollow and strange in the silent town. She was hitched in front of the cart between two long shafts; behind her hung a small lantern. The lantern seemed to tease Jamie: it shone over her back and threw dark shadows ahead of the straining dog. Jamie kept trying to jump over the shadows, but again and again she failed.

"Woof! Woof! Woof!"

Old Jake trudged along behind the cart. His hands, in thick, woolen mittens, were clenched around the handles. His cap with its crooked visor was pulled down deep over his head. His woolen scarf was bunched around his neck, and his head was drawn down between his shoulders. The cold made him shiver. Sometimes the wind whipped the powdery snow in his face.

It was quite a job for the old man to get up early every morning, rain or shine, and make the hour-long trip to the dairy farm to pick up the fresh milk he peddled door to door.

His stiff legs no longer moved as easily, and his old, worn body became very tired. But one thing was nice: his dog Jamie was an excellent cart dog, a first class dog. When she set a good pace, when she ran with her wild exuberance, pulling the old man along behind her, then Jake felt as if he could go around the world with such a dog. Her exuberant leaping and barking made the old man happy too.

"Giddy-up! Giddy-up! Attagirl!"

Through the streets they went and across the high bridge at such a daring speed that Jake almost stumbled over his own big wooden shoes. Then they were on the long, lonely country road. In the distant sky beyond the trees and beyond the dark meadows glowed a silvery light. It was the first glimmer of the new morning.

Jamie stopped when she came to the country road. She knew that now her old master would climb on the barrels to ride part of the way. She also knew that the old man would pat her on the head before he sat down: "Good Jamie; nice girl!"

"Woof! Woof!" barked the dog. She rubbed her big head lovingly against her master's trousers. "Woof! Woof!"

Then on they went again, Jamie racing along in front, the cart rumbling and swaying behind her, and Jake sitting on top of it like a king on his chariot. They flew over the road. Jamie did not let up very quickly. Her long, red tongue hung from her mouth. Her breath panted louder and louder. But she ran on for a long time without slowing down.

But old Jake did let up. He wouldn't think of tiring out a helpless animal like that. No, that would be cruel. To ride part of the way was all right. Outside of town you could ride a long ways, but if you saw that the animal was tiring, you would have to be hard-hearted indeed to go on loafing. Of course you couldn't do that!

"Stop for a minute, girl! Hold it!"

Jamie stopped. She was trembling after that fast run, and her red tongue hung from her mouth like a red flag.

Yet she turned her head toward her master, whose stiff legs almost buckled as he climbed from the cart. Her bushy tail wagged. No, too bad. This time her master didn't come to pet her. He only said, "Come on, old girl, let's go! Giddy-up!"

Well, all right then. Jamie hurried on again, but this time at a little slower pace. Old Jake trudged along behind. They went past farms still hidden by the darkness. Only the angry baying of a farm dog and the crowing of a rooster showed that people lived there. Here and there they passed small houses where the rosy light behind the curtains told of early-morning-coffee-making and of hurrying-to-get-away-in-time.

Old Jake knew every bump in this road. For many years now he had been working for the same milk dealer in town, and for many years, he had traveled this road in the early hours of the morning, whether it was cold and raw, or sunny and mild. At one time things had been better. But everything in this world changes. At one time the boss himself used to come along to pick up the milk, and they did it by horse and wagon. The boss drove, and Jake, the hired man, sat in the back between the milk barrels. At one time the boss bought milk from at least ten farmers. But that had changed too. Most farmers now made butter and cheese from the milk. That brought in more money. Only Hartman on Blue Gate Farm was still a milk producer. And now Jake had to pick up the load by himself every morning. But boy-oh-boy, at times it was very hard on him. He was past seventy now, and his life has been a life of hard work, of toil and sweat. Old Jake could feel it: he was worn out.

He was like the old milk cart which had creaked and squeaked and wobbled over the roads till, one morning, it collapsed.

But what was this? He was brooding and worrying again! He must not do that. He ought to be pleased and happy. Didn't he have a first class dog? If he didn't have Jamie to help him, then he'd have to tell Mr. Boon, "Boss, old Jake can't cut it anymore." But as long as Mr. Boon let him use this dog, he should be able to manage.

Mr. Boon didn't like Jamie. He really hated the dog. Why? She was an ugly animal. Her back sagged, her legs were crooked and turned inward, her tail was thick and shaggy and her coat coarse, and her color was very drab. This was all very true, but Boon seemed to forget that Jamie was a fine cart dog. And she was also such a warm-hearted animal. He looked only at the outside.

And that was wrong. People who looked nice on the outside weren't always the best on the inside. Then why couldn't a dog ugly on the outside be a good, courageous dog on the inside?

Deep in thought old Jake jogged along behind the cart. He didn't even notice that they were almost at the farm. Suddenly, at the bend in the road he saw the lighted window of Blue Gate Farm between the trees. With an eager howl and another "Woof!" Jamie took the corner so fast that old Jake was dragged along and lost one of his wooden shoes.

"Stop! Bad dog! Stop, I say!" As hard as he could the old man pulled back on the cart to stop it, but he had no choice but to go along. On one shoe and one sock he hopped down the soggy road "Bad dog!" he grumbled angrily.

Finally the cart stopped, and Jamie stood there trembling with eagerness to get to the farm where she would be let loose to sniff around in wonderful freedom. Old Jake had to walk back to find the lost wooden shoe. He found it on the sloping shoulder of the road. "The rascal, the ruffian!" he grumbled.

But the friendly glow of light in the window of the farmhouse on the other side of the orchard looked so tempting that Jake forgot his anger. There a hot cup of coffee awaited him, and a short rest in the warmth of the cow barn. Jake was eager to get there too.

"Giddy-up!"

The wheels crunched on the gravel of the driveway, and with a graceful turn the cart entered the farmyard.

"Stop, girl!"

The dog wiggled and squirmed so much and was so playful that Jake had a hard time freeing her, but finally with a joyful howl Jamie took off into the dark orchard. She disappeared among the tree trunks which loomed like phantoms in the grayness of the early dawn.

Jake carried the empty barrels into the cow barn and shouted, "Hello! Good morning!"

A pleasant warmth met him and embraced him. In the semi-darkness the lantern in the center of the barn looked so inviting that it seemed to say, "Come in; it's nice here." A cow mooed and stretched her head toward Jake.

A voice from the back of the stable called, "Good morning!" It was the voice of the farmhand. He was helping himself to a hot cup of coffee from the pot bubbling happily on the hot stove.

"Ah, it's nice in here! It sure is nice here!" old Jake chatted. He rubbed his hands and hunched his shoulders in quiet pleasure.

"A cup for you too, Jake?"

"Yes, please. Nothing I'd like better!"

People say that boiling coffee ruins the taste, but to Jake that didn't matter. As long as it was hot; as long as he could feel its warm glow spreading through his tired old body.

"Boy, that's great! Gives a fellow a lift."

Jake sank down on a sack of feed standing against a post. He wrapped his cold hands around the warm cup, his eyes were half closed above the steaming brew, and his nose was buried in the cup. As he sat there, he forgot his tiredness and his worries.

Outside Jamie sniffed at the door. Sure, she could come in for a while. The farmer didn't mind. The dog liked the heat too. "Lie down! Down! Don't you hear me? That's it, yes, and quiet now! Don't scare the cows."

Jamie stretched out beside the sack and looked up at her master, whose mouth, nose and eyes were completely hidden behind the white cup. She snapped at an early fly, and started to lick one of her paws. Her tail wagged restlessly. It bored Jamie to lie still.

2. Little Gertrude

In the large, cluttered kitchen of the farmhouse, someone else was also enjoying herself.

It was little Gertrude.

She was still in her petticoat and bare feet and her hair wasn't combed yet. Kneeling on a chair and bending far over the table, she dipped a rusk in a large cup of coffee. When a soggy piece broke off and splashed into the coffee, she fished it out with a spoon. It was a wonderful game she played under the lamp in the early morning. It was a game she played every morning.

Gertrude didn't like to sleep late. Mother would have liked to keep her in bed for another hour, until after the lamps were put out, but Gertrude loved to get up very early. And Gertrude was an only child. Mother found it hard to refuse her anything.

Gertrude loved that hour under the lamp. Nearby, Mother was peeling potatoes. But the table was Gertrude's kingdom. On it was a tray with a row of dirty cups that had been used earlier by the hired hand and the maids. There was a glass sugar bowl and a small tin of rock candy. There was a partly sliced loaf of bread

and a piece of bacon partly covered by a crumpled wrapper, a butter dish and a canister with rusks, and also a large chunk of cheese and a piece of sausage.

When she had eaten the rusk, little Gertrude played with two cars of an old toy train. She had tied a string to them and was carefully pulling them past the bread and the bacon and the cheese and the sausage.

The stove roared, the large teakettle sang, and some wet laundry was steaming gently on a rack near the chimney.

Her feet snugly hidden under her body, Gertrude sat in Father's easy chair. Her fumbling fingers were busy trying to fasten the string to her train. That no-good string kept coming loose whenever the train got stuck behind the piece of bacon or the canister of rusks.

From behind the kitchen door came a sudden soft sniffing and scratching. Nails scraped the wood of the door.

"What is that?" asked Mother. She was holding a freshly peeled potato in her hand, ready to drop into the pail of water at her side. Now she peered past the laundry into the shadowy corner of the kitchen.

Putting both hands on the table, Gertrude pushed herself up. She stretched her neck. "Oh, Mom, Mom! Look, a-a-a . . . ."

Slowly the door squeaked open, and through the narrow opening came a large head—the head of a dog. Two large, friendly eyes looked wonderingly into this new world that they had never seen before, and a large nose sniffed hungrily: bacon! sausage!

Mother looked startled. "Ooh! Get away, you ugly beast! Get out!"

Gertrude pressed herself against Mother. She was afraid of the big dog, but the dog's eyes were so friendly. She took a piece of bacon rind off the table and hesitantly held it out toward the dog.

But Mother shouted, "Get out!" and she threw the peeled potato at the dog. It scared the dog, and for a moment she pulled her head back behind the door. Then she reappeared and hungrily sniffed at the white thing. But dog's don't like freshly peeled potatoes.

"Oh Mom, Mom! Can I give it this? Can I? But I don't dare, Mom. Do you?"

"I don't want any animals in my kitchen. It must be Jake's dog, but how did that ugly beast get in here? Get out, you!"

"Oh, Mom! Come on, Mom!" Gertrude didn't think the dog ugly at all. It had such kind, large, brown eyes. "Come on, Mom. Let's give it something. Okay?"

"Oh, all right, I'll give her something, but not here in the kitchen. A brute like that in my kitchen? Never!"

Mother stood up. She cut a little from the piece of bacon, added some sausage skin and the piece of rind, and put it together on a plate along with some bread crusts. At heart Mother was a kind woman, and when Gertrude asked for something she could never refuse. But it would be too much to allow a strange dog into the kitchen.

"Out with you!" Bravely she stepped toward the dog, who by now had both forepaws in the kitchen. Jamie smelled the food; she danced and jumped, and spun around so eagerly that Mother almost stumbled over her. "Out with you! Calm down! Out you go!"

They went through a narrow passage to the cow barn. In a corner Mother put the plate down on the floor.

The dog attacked the food greedily.

Where was Jake? She would tell him off for not watching his dog properly. He must keep that ugly beast in check and make sure that she didn't get into her kitchen. She would give him a good tongue-lashing. But when she caught sight of the old man at the stable door, his back bent under a heavy barrel of milk, her anger melted away. What good would a scolding do? It was the first time it had ever happened, and it would probably never happen again.

Gertrude had stolen into the barn too. She was standing at the end of the passage staring at Jamie. Her eyes sparkled. "Look at those big bites!" She would like to stroke the shaggy back with her hand, but she was too afraid of the big dog.

Now look! Look at the funny faces the dog was making. A piece of bacon rind was caught between her teeth, and she couldn't get it out. Angrily she shook her head, she snorted and barked. With a clumsy paw she rubbed her snout, but she had no luck. She pranced around in anger and impatience.

It made Gertrude laugh, but at the same time she felt sorry for the dog. She would like to pull that nasty rind out from between those teeth, but—oh no!—she didn't dare! Put her hand into that big mouth? Ugh!

Outside someone rattled the chains of the harness, and a gruff voice called, "Jamie! Jamie! Come here, girl!"

The dog pricked up her ears. But there was still something left on the plate.

Gertrude heard the voice too. She wanted to tell the dog, "Listen! Someone's calling you!" But she didn't dare; she was much too frightened that the big dog would see her. Yet, carefully she went a step or two closer.

"Jamie! Here girl!" barked a voice nearby. "Where are you?"

Jamie forgot the bothersome thing between her teeth. With a few big bites she tried to empty her plate. But the rind clung to her tongue, and she could hardly swallow. With an angry bark she jumped backward. Her big, bushy tail hit Gertrude square in the face.

Oh! Ugh! That tail frightened Gertrude. She fell back against the wall of the barn. Then she raced away back down the passage and into the kitchen. Fearfully she slammed the door. Ugh! That horrid tickling of all those hairs! Ugh!

"Come on, lazybones, where are you? Ah, there you are!" Jake found his lost dog. Seizing her by the collar, he dragged her out of the barn. Jamie snorted and gagged and pulled back.

"What's the matter with you, you big lug? What's wrong? Aha! There's something stuck between your teeth, is there? Come here, girl; let me take it out."

That made Jamie feel better! With that nasty thing gone from her mouth, she forgot all about the leftovers on the plate. Willingly she allowed herself to be harnessed, pawing the ground impatiently.

In the back of the barn, at the end of the narrow

passage, the kitchen door opened a crack. Gertrude listened, and then fearfully she stuck her head of tousled hair through the opening. "Giddy-up!" she heard in the distance. There was a hoarse bark, and wheels crunched in the gravel. Then the yard was quiet again.

Gertrude stepped into the maid's big wooden shoes and went in search of Mother to tell her the horrible story of the big, bushy tail.

3. Her Real Master

"Who owns that dog—me or you? Tell me!"

"Sure, boss, you do. But, you see, I take her out every morning, and I know her very well. If you only knew how faithful and friendly she is! She's never stubborn or mean. No, when I take her out, she's always willing to work hard. But, you see, boss, if she's teased—"

"Teased, nothing! What do you know? She's my dog and if I want to kick her or beat her, I don't need your permission. Is that understood, Jake? I have a mind to tie a rock around her neck and throw her into the canal. Then she can no longer track up the store with her dirty paws or snap at little Johnny when he playfully squeezes her ears with the plyers. Ha-ha-ha! And you, I won't have you siding with that animal. Or else you can go, too! Who do you think you are? Me and Johnny boy—we're the boss around here, and we'll do with the dog as we please. You're only the hired hand, and you can keep your mouth shut!"

Old Jake bowed his head and closed his eyes. He didn't want to see or hear anything more. He stooped forward over the barrels in the yard behind the store and picked up a brush to scour them.

Mr. Boon, still furious at the dog for biting Johnny's shirt, hurled the heavy wooden plug from a milk barrel against Jamie's head and roared, "Get into the dog house, you mutt!"

Jamie whined and slunk back, her tail between her legs. Hiding deep in her house, she tried to lick her ear. It was bleeding and very painful. The little boy had hurt her badly today with his plyers.

Again she tried to lick her ear, but she didn't have much luck. Then she rubbed it with her paw. When that didn't help, she lay down and rested her aching head on her paws. With the bleeding ear on the floor she tried to endure the pain. She stared out into the yard with her large, brown eyes. From the dog house she could see Jake's wide pantlegs and his dirty wooden shoes.

Two or three times she hesitantly stood up. She would like to push her painful ear against those pantlegs and lie down close to those dirty wooden shoes. With Jake she would find comfort, and safety, and help. Jamie wanted to do that, but she didn't dare. Jamie understood very little of the world of people. But one thing she did understand: the best spot in the world for her was close to old Jake.

Earlier, when the boss had kicked and beaten her, she had fled to old Jake too, almost bowling him over. Then old Jake had talked and talked, but not at her. And the boss had talked too. His voice had become louder and louder, and angrier and angrier. Finally he had thrown something hard against her head. Why

hadn't old Jake stopped him? Was old Jake scared too? How could that be?

Jamie was scared of everyone: of the boss, who always wore heavy shoes with cleats; of Neil, the young hired man who often took her out with the cart to deliver milk to the customers in town, and who always took a stick along; and of little Johnny who always teased her, who laughed loudly when he hurt her, and who ran to his father whenever Jamie growled and showed her teeth. She was afraid of all those people. But she wasn't afraid of Jake. When those others said something, she obeyed because she was afraid of them, but when old

Jake said something she obeyed gladly. They were all her masters—the boss, Neil, little Johnny—but Jake was the master of all the masters.

Yes, Jamie's small mind understood little of the world of humans. She understood only a few of their words: "Giddy-up!" and "Good girl!" and "Good Jamie!" and a few others which Jake often said. But she understood very well what old Jake told her with his eyes.

Jamie loved Jake with all the loyalty a dog's heart could muster. Jamie didn't know that Mr. Boon at one time had paid money for her, and that therefore the evil tempered man was her real master. Because old Jake loved her, and she loved old Jake, she thought that old Jake was her real master.

Faithfully every morning the two went out into the world: Jamie in front and Jake behind the cart, like two faithful friends.

They even looked like each other. They were both ugly. They were both easily frightened. They were both content with little, and they both soon forgot when someone hurt them. They were both plodders who had to work hard and who seldom heard a kind word. When Jake was scolded or when people snapped at him, he bowed his head and remained silent. When Jamie was kicked or beaten, she put her tail between her legs and slunk away.

Neither Jake nor Jamie had a pleasant life. But early in the morning when it was still dark, and they raced along the lonely road, when they were together with no one to bother them, then the whole world belonged to them. The trip to Blue Gate Farm was the high point of their day.

Whenever they rounded the bend in the road and caught sight of the farm behind the trees, there was always a silent joy in their hearts. Jake always got his cup of coffee, and sometimes—when the farmer's wife was in a good mood—a bowlful of porridge, and he could rest his old, worn-out body in the warm barn for a while. Jamie got her freedom, and she could sniff around for something to eat: a misplaced soupbone or a ham rind.

Mr. Hartman was a well-to-do farmer. He was a nice enough fellow, but it made no difference to him who came to pick up his milk. He wouldn't harm those two plodders who were there every morning, but he wouldn't go out of his way to be good to them, either. Sometimes he made them wait a long time, and sometimes only a little while. Then off they went again. That was the way it should be. Farmer Hartman never gave them a second thought. Why should he? If another man and another dog came to pick up the milk tomorrow, that would be fine with him. As long as his milk got picked up.

Mrs. Hartman was a more thoughtful, kinder person. She sometimes thought of Jake, and she would give him a piece of bacon to take home, or when they had slaughtered a pig, a few pork chops. But she never thought of Jamie. What did that dog matter to her? She was an ugly animal, and on the farm there were plenty of animals she had to think of: cows and horses and ducks and chickens. They didn't have a dog. At one time they had had one, but they could do without. The fewer worries she had, the better she liked it. But Mrs. Hartman was very changeable. One day she might be friendly, but the next day she might be in a bad mood and act surly and gruff.

Little Gertrude's life as a child amidst all the hustle and bustle of the farm was a happy one. She didn't know that some people were poor, and others rich. She knew nothing of worry and sadness. She was really a little spoiled, because as an only child she nearly always got her way. But little Gertrude had a heart that was easily moved to pity and she didn't like to see others mistreated.

On the morning that Jamie had sniffed his way into the kitchen, and had boldly stuck her head around the door, little Gertrude had spoken up for her. It had brought the dog a plateful of delicious snacks and a tough piece of rind between her teeth. The little girl had been badly frightened when Jamie's thick, bushy tail had tickled her face. But now, the next morning, she was there again, behind her mother, behind the wet laundry, behind the cluttered table with the bread, the bacon, the cups and the tins, waiting to see if Jamie would come to scratch at the door again.

But as she waited she suddenly heard loud noises in the narrow passage on the other side of the door. Startled, she squeezed her mother's arm and hastily climbed on her lap, right on top of the potatoes. She thought that at least a hundred large dogs with thick, bushy tails were about to come racing through the door. Pails clattered on the cement floor, a deep voice shouted threats, and above all this clamor sounded the frightened whining of a dog.

Then the door opened and Father came in. He was still laughing.

"What was that?" Mother asked wonderingly.

"Ha-ha-ha!" laughed the farmer. "That ugly dog of old Jake was sniffing at our door, and just for fun I threw those two old milk pails after her and yelled, 'Hey you!' Did I ever scare her! She almost keeled over. Ha-ha-ha!"

"Oh, Dad!" fretted Gertrude. She was half angry and half sad. Now the dog wouldn't come to the door anymore. Suddenly she felt sorry for Jamie.

But Father didn't even hear her. He was far too busy. And Mother didn't listen either. "That dog had it coming. She was getting too bold. And Jake just lets her roam. But after this she'll stay away for a while."

Gertrude slipped away: out the door, through the narrow passage, into the cow barn. She couldn't find any wooden shoes, so on her stocking feet, she cautiously tiptoed ahead to see where Jamie had gone. She was afraid; if the dog suddenly rushed up to her, she would be terribly frightened. The farther she went, the slower she walked. She wasn't afraid of all those big cows mooing, shaking their heads, and rattling their chains, but a large, strange, fierce dog . . . .

She caught sight of old Jake. He was sitting behind a wooden partition. His hands were folded and he had his cap off; it was gripped between his thumbs. His bald, gleaming head fringed by silver hair was bowed. Jake was saying grace. Beside him, on an upside down pail, stood a steaming cup of coffee, and on his knees lay the small gingham sack in which he always carried his breakfast.

Jamie was sitting close to him. She held her head high, and her large, brown eyes were fixed on Jake's moving lips and his closed eyes. Very slowly and hesitantly, she put a heavy, clumsy paw on Jake's knee, right next to the gingham sack, as if to say, "Why are you keeping your eyes closed for so long? I'm hungry for a snack."

Little Gertrude forgot her fear. Nearer and nearer she went. She stood still, her hands behind her back, her nose turned up, her eyes fixed on old Jake in glad expectation.

Finally Jake's eyes slowly opened. He put his cap back on and pulled it deep down over his gray hair. Then he took a sandwich from the gingham sack.

"Hello, little girl. Coming for a visit?"

Gertrude blushed, not so much because old Jake talked to her, but because Jamie looked at her with those big eyes and turned around and sniffed at her skirt. Gertrude was frightened and put both hands to her mouth.

Jake saw her fear.

"Come here, you beggar! Do you want a bite, too?" Jamie forgot about the child and opened her mouth to catch the offered snack.

"Give me a paw first, old girl!"

Jamie jumped up, put both paws in Jake's outstretched hand, and stuck her wet nose into the open sack.

"No, no, do it politely if you want something!"

Jamie sat down again; with her head cocked and a grave face, she solemnly put a clumsy paw in Jake's hand.

"Attagirl!"

A small piece of Jake's sandwich dropped into the dog's wide open mouth and disappeared in one hungry swallow. Another piece followed, and another. "The poor animal," thought Jake. "She doesn't get much to eat at home, and an old fellow like me no longer needs much."

Open-mouthed, her eyes sparkling with pleasure, little Gertrude looked on. She had a wonderful thought, but it was very dangerous. Finally she dared to ask it, "Can I ... can I do it too?"

"Of course, sweetheart. Come, step this way. Here's a piece. No, no, don't let her take it yet. First she must shake hands with you very politely. Come on, girl, give her a nice paw."

Little Gertrude trembled. The big dog suddenly lifted one of her horrible, hairy paws, and put it on her hand. Oh, she wanted to squeeze her eyes shut and pull her hand away. It was so scary, but ... it was nice too. Jamie's paw touched her hand only for a moment. Then, glad that it was done, the girl tossed the bite Jake had given her at Jamie. It hit her on the nose.

Away Gertrude ran back to the kitchen, to Mother. Stuttering in haste, she told Mother about the nice dog and her own daring. And she asked, she begged, she

whined—she had to have a piece of bread for Jamie, who was still so terribly hungry.

Mother grumbled a little. Mother let her wait a little, but Gertrude got her way. Mother gave her a thick slice of bread. Gertrude herself snatched some sausage ends from the table and put all the goodies in her skirt. Holding the skirt with both hands, she ran back to the barn, almost tripping over the ends of her sagging stockings.

"Look what I've got!" she shouted gleefully.

And all at once she dropped all the goodies at Jamie's feet.

That was how Jamie had another good morning.

4. Shattered Peace

It was a sunny Sunday morning in the summertime.

Blue Gate Farm, with its carefully raked drive, its scrubbed steps, and its newly washed walk of yellow bricks, lay hidden behind the dense leaves of the trees. It was very quiet around the farm. A lonely finch warbled in the walnut tree, flitted down on the lane, and hopped through the spots of golden sunlight which fell through the trees.

That neatly raked drive was marred a little by the tracks of a two-wheeled cart and between them the footprints of a dog. Jake and Jamie had done that.

Like every other morning, they came and disappeared into the cow barn. The milk cart was waiting at the meadow gate, where the pailfuls of milk would be poured into the barrels. Jake was waiting in the barn. Everything was spotlessly clean inside, and it was nice and cool. Rush mats were propped against the posts to which the cows were tied during the winter, forming a yellow partition. Jake liked his cup of coffee in the summertime too. Jamie was with him, as always hungry for a snack.

The barn door opened a crack.

It was very quiet on Blue Gate Farm that sunny Sunday morning in the summertime.

In the summer kitchen, the small room next to the barn which the Hartman family used as long as the cattle were out in the field, it was not quiet. Dressed in her Sunday best, a golden necklace about her neck and golden rings in her ears, Mrs. Hartman rushed about. It was very early, but she was going to church, and that was an hour's walk from the farm. She wanted to leave in time, for she couldn't stand it when she had to hurry in the summer heat. Little Gertrude was going with her. She was wearing a bright red dress with a yellow check, and her white hat was topped with colorful flowers. Yes, they were going to church, but there was much to do before they could leave.

"Yes, Jake, as you can see there's never any rest for a person on a farm."

Old Jake, seated on a chair against the wall, was having his second cup of coffee. "Yes, Mrs. Hartman, what should I say? When the good Lord gives us health, it doesn't matter so much. People who don't like their work cannot be happy."

"You, you old workhorse, you're always content. I wish I were like that. Come, let me pour you another cup! What's that? Don't you even have a piece of cheese on your bread on Sunday? My, my, nothing but a scratch of butter. Here, let me treat you."

The farmer's wife cut a couple of thick slices of cheese and put them on Jake's bread. And she wrapped a piece of sausage in some paper and pushed it toward Jake: "Here, put that in your sack for tonight!"

She was in a very good mood this morning. Was it because it was Sunday, or because of the bright sunshine outside, or because of her pretty Sunday dress, or because of the pleasant walk that lay ahead? Or was it because of all these things together? Jake didn't know, but she was in a good mood. She had called him inside this morning, too, something she seldom did.

"How long has your wife been dead now, Jake?"

"It will be fifteen years this coming Christmas."

"That's a long time! And do you still live in that room by yourself?"

"Well, yes. I'm in my seventies now, and I won't be here much longer. I'll be happy when the Lord God calls me. Then I'll see my wife again, and my little girl too. She's been dead for thirty-three years. When she died she was just about the age of your little girl. She was also an only child, and we never had any other children.

It was a sad story, and Mrs. Hartman would rather not hear sad stories on this happy Sunday morning.

"What do you want now, child?" she asked Gertrude who was begging for something to give to the dog for the third time. "Oh, is it the same story. Is your darling dog still hungry? Well, here then. Bring her this, but watch you don't break my nice plate! Wait a minute, I have a delicious hambone for her."

Away ran Gertrude.

"Gertrude, Gertrude!" Mother called after her. "Come right back, you hear! Don't get your good dress dirty. And be careful with that plate!"

Gertrude came right back. She was seldom disobedient.

The world was beautiful that sunny Sunday morning, and there was joy everywhere! Jake enjoyed his thick slices of cheese and his fourth cup of coffee with a thankful heart. The sun was shining in the big, beautiful world outside, and its friendly light came through the window into the small room of the farmhouse. It sent a golden beam across Jake's knees and across his rugged, wrinkled hand. The golden sunshine reminded him of sunny mornings, long ago, when his wife and his little girl were still alive. But the golden sunshine also reminded him of the everlasting morning that was coming, when light would never again turn into darkness and when happiness would never die.

Mrs. Hartman gathered together everything she needed for church: the Psalter with its golden clasp; her clean, neatly folded handkerchief; her black gloves; her crystal bottle of cologne with its golden cap; some peppermints in a crumpled piece of paper; and her beaded purse with the silver frame. She counted her money; the cheerful morning made her so glad that she put a couple of large shiny coins into a separate compartment: they were for the collection bag.

Little Gertrude in her clean dress and her flowery hat was making a bouquet out of the soft, white duck feathers she had gathered in the orchard earlier that morning. Later she would ask Mother to pin the feathers to her hat, next to the colorful flowers. That would make the hat even more beautiful.

Farmer Hartman and his hired man were approaching in the pasture, carrying heavy pails full of foaming milk. "Hi, Jake. Beautiful morning, isn't it? We'll light up a nice cigar to celebrate it. We've earned it, don't you think?"

"Yes, boss, and thanks."

In the big walnut tree the birds were also celebrating the sunshine.

There was joy and happiness everywhere!

Crash!

Suddenly a strange, crashing sound, a horrible sound, shattered the peaceful morning. The peace and joy of the morning seemed to crack with the sound.

Jake sat up with a start. He spilled coffee on his sunny knee.

Mrs. Hartman dropped a coin into the wrong compartment and listened. "What's that?"

After much trouble little Gertrude squeezed all her feathers together into one warm hand; suddenly she lost half of them again.

Mr. Hartman and the hired man didn't hear much of the crash. Their milk pails made too much of a clatter. But a finch, pecking at some oats near the open barn door, fled in fear; it flew through the empty hayrack to the safety of the orchard.

Suddenly Mrs. Hartman flung down her purse on top of all her other things, and the cheerfulness fled from her face. It darkened just like the sunny world darkens when heavy thunderclouds hide the sun. She snapped at old Jake as if it was his fault, "I hope that ugly dog of yours didn't break my nice . . . ." And she ran out the door into the barn.

Startled, old Jake stumbled after her.

And little Gertrude forgot her feathers and hurried after them.

The tall, broad shape of Mr. Hartman appeared in the open barn door, blocking the cheerful sunlight. His hired man looked on from behind.

Close to the barn door, in a golden beam of sunlight, lay the smashed plate. Over it stood Jamie with the hambone in her mouth. She looked about her as if to say, "Let anyone try to touch my goodies!" The rest of her food lay on the floor with the splintered plate.

"You dumb dog! You clumsy mutt!" scolded Mrs. Hartman. "My plate! It belongs to my good set! Oh, I could . . . I could . . . ! Out, I say! Get out, you brute! And she delivered a painful kick with her beautiful, shiny shoe. Mr. Hartman took out the buggy whip and the hired man grabbed the broom. "Get out, you mutt! Out!" The whip snapped and the broom whacked down on Jamie's back.

Unnerved by the fierce attack, the dog fled. Through the door she went across the yard to hide between the wheels of the milk cart. There she lay trembling in fear. Her dog-pleasure was spoiled, but she did save one thing—the hambone. It lay between her paws, and she growled softly. Armed with his broom, the hired man tried to play the hero; he walked up to the dog to take the bone away. But the dog growled angrily, and the otherwise friendly, brown eyes flashed dangerously, so he didn't dare.

After Jamie had fled the barn, all the anger was turned on old Jake. It was his fault. Why did he allow that dog to run loose on the yard? Why didn't he tie her to the gate?

That greedy dog had dragged the plate with food from the far corner of the barn, and now it lay here at the door smashed to pieces. Why did that dog have to drag the plate around? Why didn't old Jake keep his eyes on her?

"Sorry, folks," Jake said softly. "You're right, of course. But what can I say? She's only an animal."

"But I won't have an animal smashing my good plates," snapped Mrs. Hartman. She rearranged the heavy, golden necklace. "I ought to let you pay for it! That mutt! That . . . !"

"I'll pay for the plate if you wish. But I understand why the dog dragged that plate to the door. She's got three pups at home, and she must have wanted to take the food to her young ones. Just look: everything is there yet. She hasn't taken anything for herself."

"Just sweep that mess up," grumbled the farmer. Jake swept. What a pity that the dumb dog had to spoil the beautiful morning. But was he angry at the dog? No, he wasn't. In her animal ignorance, she didn't mean any harm.

Once more Jake tried to soothe Mrs. Hartman. "You take good care of your little girl, and so did I of mine when she was alive. That dog only wanted to look after her young."

"Oh, you! A dog is only a dog. If she were human it would be a different story. Don't try to excuse her!" Angrily she walked away after her husband.

"What a shame!" mumbled Jake. "Now all the joy, all the beauty of this morning is broken in pieces, just like this plate." He walked up to Jamie, took the hambone away from her, and put it on the cart. She would get it back when they got home.

Jamie didn't growl at him.

As the cart left crunching over the sunlit lane, from under a flowery Sunday hat a girl's face peered through a crack in the barn door. Her eyes didn't look happy; those kind, blue eyes were big and warm with pity. All the shouting and yelling had frightened little Gertrude. And when she had seen Father bring his whip down on Jamie's back, and the hired man brandish the broom, she had squeezed her eyes closed in fear.

"Oh, no, Daddy! No!" she had cried, but her small, high voice had been lost among all those loud noises.

Now she watched Jamie go. Poor Jamie hadn't eaten anything herself and had nothing to take to her pups either.

Little Gertrude whispered, "But I love you anyhow!" And her lips grew firm as she thought of what she would do. "When you come again, I'll ask for something to eat for you anyway."

With Jamie in front and Jake behind it, the cart rattled over the sunny country road toward home. This morning Jake didn't sit on the barrels at all. Make the animal slave on top of it all? No, Jake couldn't do that. He would rather get a little more tired himself! Later he was going to church, and there, on his seat in the corner

where he faithfully sat every Sunday morning, he would
have a chance to rest. There he could listen and think in
peace; there no one bothered him; there no one shouted
or quarreled; there God Himself spoke to Jake. And the
old man longed for that quiet hour.

"Giddy-up, girl!"

Jamie sped up a little, but her heart wasn't in it. The
cart swerved along the road as if she had forgotten how
to run fast and straight. Jamie's small dog's mind
couldn't understand the people in her world.

Old Jake just plodded along. He was thinking, and he
mumbled to himself, "You poor, dumb dog! You don't
understand why people act so strange. You don't understand that they get angry when you break a plate. To
you a plate is just a white, slippery thing that you can't
hold between your teeth. You don't understand why
they scolded you and beat you when you didn't mean to
do anything bad. You see, Jamie, you're a dumb dog!

"No, girl, people don't easily forgive you when you
do something wrong. They want to be forgiven
whenever they do something wrong. But people want an
animal, a dumb beast, always to be obedient and do
exactly what they're told, or else they kick and beat the
animal, because it's only a beast. But what about themselves—what are they?

"Giddy-up! Yes, yes, at home I'll chop that nice
hambone in pieces so you can really enjoy it. Your pups
won't like it, though."

When the dog saw the first houses of the town, she
began to run a little faster. Her wet tongue dangled from
her panting mouth.

Jake mused on, "If our Master on high hit us whenever we did something wrong, and if He refused to forgive us, then it would go bad with all of us."

In one of the cottages along the road a woman opened her curtains just as Jake went by. When she saw him look upward, she wondered if he was expecting rain on this sunny Sunday morning.

But old Jake wasn't looking at the sky. He was looking up to heaven. And in his heart he prayed, "Lord Jesus, forgive all of us our sins. Forgive me too! And teach us to forgive and forget when others sin against us."

5. Where Is Gertrude?

The beautiful summer was over. As the two milk haulers made their way to Blue Gate Farm through the gray fall mornings, yellow leaves fluttered down from the trees, riding along between the barrels, in the pockets of Jake's old coat, or on Jamie's bushy tail. Some days the fall rains made Jamie's broad paws slip on the slippery road. Both of them, however, still looked forward to arriving at Blue Gate Farm every morning. Someone with very little say on the farm, but who nearly always got her way, made sure of that.

Little Gertrude had kept her word: "I love you anyhow! When you come again, I'll ask for something to eat for you!"

She did so faithfully every day. Yes, she took better care of Jamie than of Jake. Jamie was really the only one she took care of. But Jake didn't mind. "At least there's somebody who cares for you, even if she's just a little girl," he often thought when little Gertrude showed up carrying a plateful of bread, or a dish with bones, or some other doggy snack. He had to hold the thankful dog back—sometimes by the tail—so she wouldn't bowl over the happy, bright-eyed child. It gladdened Jake's heart to see it, so he, too, enjoyed the time spent waiting at Blue Gate Farm. The story of the broken plate was long forgotten.

It wasn't always easy for Gertrude to take care of her friend. When Mother was in a good mood, and that was usually, it went fine, but when Mother was in a bad mood, Gertrude had to wheedle, using her sweetest voice and clinging to Mother's skirt until Mother gave her something for Jamie.

"That bothersome dog! I wish I had never seen her!" Mother might grumble while she found some stale bread, or some rinds, or a few bones. But then Gertrude would look at her with her charmingly naughty eyes, put her arms tightly around Mother's neck, and chatter, "I love Jamie very much, and I love you very much too, Mom." And suddenly Mother's bad mood would disappear.

"You little chit, you're nothing but a flatterer!" Mother said smiling. "You ought to go home with Jake and Jamie so you can always take care of that dog."

By then little Gertrude wasn't listening anymore. She was already getting something for Jamie; that was what counted. She waited while the dog gulped down the food, taking big, greedy bites. She even dared to hold the gruesome, hairy tail. Later they both roamed around the farm and the orchard. Nobody knew what all little Gertrude told Jamie; maybe even Jamie didn't know.

But one gray fall morning, when the wet leaves stuck

to the road and to the wheels of the milk cart, when Jake entered the barn shivering with cold, and Jamie followed him with her dirty paws and glistening, wet coat, Gertrude was not there.

Mr. Hartman was out in the field. Mrs. Hartman walked through the stable, barely nodding in reply to Jake's friendly "Good morning!" Her face was so gloomy that the old man didn't dare to ask where the little girl was.

Jamie always had to stay with her master till Gertrude came. Impatiently she lifted her head and sniffed the air. Finally she couldn't restrain her longing for her morning snack any longer.

"Woof! Woof!" she barked in a deep voice, as if to say, "Come on! Where are you this morning? Don't you know that I'm terribly hungry?" But Jake tapped her on the head: "Quiet, girl. What's the noise all about? Be patient! She'll come."

But the girl didn't come.

When her master wasn't looking, Jamie went sniffing around the barn. Time after time she stopped at the narrow passage leading to the kitchen, as if she knew, "She's in there. I can smell her. Why doesn't she come out?"

Jake was looking too. He looked outside the barn. Perhaps she was with one of the maids in the pig barn or in the carriage house and hadn't heard the milk cart coming. Jake couldn't find the little girl.

But Jamie could . . . .

When the old man came back to the barn and sat down in his usual corner to wait for the cup of coffee which one of the maids would soon bring him, the dog was nowhere to be seen. "Well, she'll show up again. She must have come after me and is now roaming around the yard somewhere.

"My chest . . . . Whew, my chest sure hurts today! Yes, this old cart is beginning to squeak badly."

In the passage by the kitchen door, a dog's nose sniffed cautiously. Then it pushed, pushed . . . until the door creaked open. The sound startled Jamie. She jumped back with her tail between her legs. But nothing happened. No threatening voices or kicking feet came through the open door, and no one threw any clattering pails at her.

She tried again. She pushed and pushed . . . until all of her head was in the kitchen. She saw no one. But little Gertrude must be there. Jamie could smell her. So Jamie kept searching for her.

It was very dangerous. Fearfully, her ears flat and her tail tucked between her legs, she crept forward. Danger seemed to be lurking everywhere. But she smelled Gertrude; she must find Gertrude.

Now Jamie was inside all the way. She sniffed the air; she sniffed the floor. The trail led farther. Her broad, dirty paws walked across the beautiful rug close to the table. On the table, in the center of the red tablecloth, stood a small bottle on a plate. There was also a glass with a spoon in it. What could it be? Was it something good to eat? Did it smell good?

Standing up on her hind legs, Jamie put her heavy forepaws on the table. She forgot her fear and stretched her head as far as she could toward the plate and the glass. Ugh! She had never before smelled anything as bad as this. When she lowered herself to the floor again, the table shook. The bottle tipped over on the plate, and the smelly medicine splashed from the glass. Now beside the dirty prints left by Jamie's paws, there were also medicine stains on the tablecloth.

Jamie went to the other side of the table and sniffed again. She must be on the right track. She could smell Gertrude more plainly now. Ah! There was an open door on the other side of the kitchen. It led to a small, dark room. In the darkness stood a bed, and in that bed . . . ?

The large paws went clack-clack-clack on the polished floor. Jamie stuck her head through the open door.

Brrr! Gertrude had been very cold and had had a terrible headache when she began to get up that morning. Last night, too, she had shivered with cold and her teeth had chattered. "You're sick, Gertrude," Mother had said. "You better get back into bed, and stay nice and warm today. I'll give you some medicine and make you some nice soup. Tomorrow you'll probably be better again."

Gertrude let Mother put her back in bed; her head felt so heavy and hurt so badly that she wanted nothing so much as to put it down on the pillow, close her eyes tightly, and go back to sleep. Mother tucked her in warmly, fetched another blanket from the big bed, and covered the sick child with it. The woolly thing tickled Gertrude's cheek a little, but it was nice and warm.

Little Gertrude had gone back to sleep.

The family still used the summer kitchen, but in another week the cows would come back to the barn, and Mother would move back into the big kitchen. But now it was still clean and very quiet. The floor was spotless, and everything gleamed and sparkled.

As she slept, Gertrude was walking down a long, dark road. She met a milk cart drawn by a large dog, followed by another one, and another one, and another. There must have been a hundred milk carts with large dogs. It was very dark, and all the dogs were coming toward her. Oh, she was so frightened. They were all walking backward, and they all had bushy tails, and they pushed their gruesome, hairy tails into her face, into her eyes, into her mouth, into her nose. Oh, she wanted to scream, but she couldn't. She thrashed around with her arms. Ah, Mother was coming. Look how scared those dogs with their hairy tails were! Off they ran, the teasers. Yes, when Mother came they were afraid!

But now all those poor dogs got nothing to eat. They must not go hungry. But Mother was coming. She would know what to do. She always knew what to do. Gertrude didn't dare to give them anything. She was much too frightened. If only old Jake were here, but he had left with all the milk carts and the barrels. Where did he go?

Oh, but there was Mother now, and she hugged little Gertrude and kissed her. But why was Mother's nose so cold and wet? And when Gertrude stroked Mother's cheeks, they felt hairy. Mother kissed her, and Mother loved her very much. Mother's tongue was very long, and she put her long tongue against Gertrude's cheek. And Mother was panting.

Mother put her arm around Gertrude. That was nice. But why was her arm so hard? If felt like . . . like a piece of wood, or like . . . like a dog's paw. Mom, oh Mom, why are you acting so strange?

"Woof!"

Horrors, what was that? What was it?

Little Gertrude sat up with a sudden start. That terrible sound close to her ears made her shudder in fear. And then . . . then she saw. It wasn't Mother who had hugged and kissed her. It had been a big dog nose that had sniffed her ear; it had been a long dog tongue which had licked her cheek; it had been a hard dog paw that had hugged her; and it had been a big, open dog mouth that had barked so horribly close.

But her fear died down as she saw that it was Jamie standing beside her bed and looking at her with large, happy eyes that seemed to say, "Look, I had no trouble finding you!" Gertrude fell back on the pillow. It had been a bad dream! The woolen blanket tickled her face. The hairy tails of her dream had been the fuzz of the blanket.

But Jamie didn't like to see Gertrude crawl back under the blankets. She pawed the covers as if to say, "What's the matter with you? Come on, get up. Aren't you going to get me something nice to eat?"

Gertrude laughed, and she slid down even deeper under the blankets until she was almost completely hidden. Jamie became impatient. She stuck her nose between the blankets and the pillow to find that teasing face. She sniffed and snorted, and her long tongue lapped Gertrude's nose when the girl peeked out for a moment. "Bah! Bad dog!" she grumbled. "Go away! Get!" But she wasn't really angry. She put her head back on the pillow and pulled Jamie's big head down beside her. This was like Little Red Riding Hood in the picture book: the big wolf with his ugly head and his large mouth full of white teeth lying in grandmother's bed. But that wolf wore a large, white bonnet. Jamie should have a bonnet too. Gertrude looked around; one of Mother's bonnets would fit Jamie.

But then . . . quick footsteps came through the narrow passage into the kitchen, and an angry and surprised voice exclaimed, "What is this? Who made those dirty tracks on my good rug? And how did that mud get on my table? And the bottle is tipped over!"

Jamie jumped back in alarm. She peeked around the corner into the kitchen. Gertrude wasn't frightened at all. She knew that it was Mother's voice, and she called, "Come back here, Jamie!"

Mother raised both hands in anger and astonishment. "What? Are you in here, you filthy dog? Did you dirty my kitchen? Out, I say! Out!"

Mother didn't see any other weapon to use on the intruder, so she pulled one slipper from her foot and attacked Jamie. "Get out, you mutt! Out!"

Jamie was terrified. She had been threatened by angry words and empty pails and whips and brooms and sticks so often, she knew all the dangers. And now she was caught in a small, dark room. She slunk to a corner

and made herself as small as possible. She tried to hide under Gertrude's bed, but her body was far too bulky. "Get out, ugly beast!"

"No, Mom! No!" yelled Gertrude. She climbed on top of her pillow to see where Jamie was. "Mom!"

But Mother didn't hear her. She saw the dirty stains of Jamie's muddy paws on the clean, white sheets and on Gertrude's nightgown, and she flew into a rage. Slap! Slap! the slipper went on the back of the cringing dog. Jamie whined in fear. Suddenly she dashed away, passing so close to Mother that she fell against the bed. Jamie was free. She rounded the corner into the kitchen so fast that her nails skidded on the polished floor and slued the rug to the side. She raced through the kitchen so fast that she pulled the tablecloth half off the table. Out the door and through the narrow passage she fled.

Mother's slipper followed her, but it missed.

"Why, Mom? Why?"

"Look, child! Look how that ugly dog made everything dirty. Didn't that beast scare you? Get back under the covers, quickly! That dog is going to make you even sicker than you are."

"But Mom, we were playing Little Red Riding Hood, and now . . . . Can she come back for a while, Mom?"

"Come back? What an idea! Of course not! Just stay under the blankets. In a little while I'll boil you an egg."

Mother hopped about on her one slipper. Still grumbling, she straightened the rug and the tablecloth, angrily shaking her head at the ugly scratches the fleeing Jamie made on the nicely polished floor. "That ugly beast!"

"Mother! Mom!" Gertrude called from the bedroom. "Aren't you going to give Jamie anything to eat this morning?"

Mother grumbled, "Give her something? I'd like to give her a beating!" Still very angry, she walked away down the passage.

Gertrude was left alone. She was sad. She didn't understand Mother's anger. Now the poor dog wouldn't get anything because she—Gertrude—was sick. That was unfair. But tomorrow, when she was better again, and the day after tomorrow, and all the other tomorrows as long as she lived, she would make sure that Jamie didn't go hungry. That poor Jamie!

Mother was very angry with the dog, but when she was at work again in the summer kitchen, she still heard Gertrude's sad little voice asking, "Aren't you going to give Jamie anything this morning?" Well, there were some leftovers from yesterday's dinner; she would give that to the dog. But it wasn't because she loved that ugly brute so much. Not at all! It was because she loved sick little Gertrude so much. That was why.

Mrs. Hartman fetched the dish of leftovers, but when she came to the barn, she heard the wheels of the milk cart crunching on the gravel drive. Her kindness had come too late.

They made the return trip at a steady trot. Jamie enjoyed the run. Jamie ran with pleasure. She had a good morning after all: she had eaten most of Jake's breakfast because Jake hadn't been hungry. Old Jake was sitting on top of the barrels. He didn't feel well. His chest hurt, and he was shivering with cold. What if he became sick?

"Sorry, old girl," he mumbled sadly, "but this morning your old master is going to ride all the way home. My legs are so shaky. Giddy-up! Keep it up, girl! You won't have to drag me along very often anymore. Old Jake is wearing out."

Jamie ran on. She barked at a farm dog which yapped at her from behind a closed gate, and she swerved sharply when a frightened hen burst cackling from a hedge in front of her. She wasn't tired.

Now they were at the high bridge.

"But when I can't go with you in the morning," old Jake mumbled worriedly, "who will be your master then?"

6. The Willow Switch

Everything in the world changes.

Today the sun smiles down on the happy fields, but tomorrow . . . ?

Today there is joy and gladness, but tomorrow . . . ?

Today two friends find pleasure in each other's company, but tomorrow . . . ?

Everything in the world changes.

In the gray morning the milk cart clattered through the dark, lonely streets of the town. It was traveling very fast.

"Faster, I said! Move it!" A long willow switch cracked against the wheels and lashed across Jamie's back. With a frightened lurch the dog ran still faster. But not for long. Even a horse couldn't keep up such speed. But Jamie had to keep it up. Neil demanded it. And again the switch lashed down. "Faster, I say! You lazy mutt! Move it!"

Up the bridge they went and down the other side at a furious speed. Ah! Neil's eyes sparkled. This was what he liked. "Faster! Move it!"

Jamie stumbled. The heavy cart pushed her forward, grazing her head and her paws on the frozen ground.

"Come on, you ugly mutt, get up!"

Crack! Crack!

With several nasty whacks and a rough tug at the handle, Neil prodded the dog up again. He jumped on the barrels, brandished the switch in the air, and yelled, "Move it! Run! Faster!"

"He'd teach that lazy dog! A thin, lashing willow switch can work wonders. He'd make that dog run until her tongue dragged on the ground. That was good for lazy dogs. Jake, that old goat, had always treated her as if she were a pet. But now Jamie would learn otherwise. Neil would show that he knew how to teach an old dog new tricks. He'd make her run until she couldn't go another step.

Crack! Crack!

What if the dog ran herself to death? Neil didn't think of that, and when he did he shrugged, "She's only an ugly mutt, and Boon has plenty of money to buy another dog, a much better one."

Did that dog think their morning trip to the Blue Gate Farm was a pleasure drive? Neil scowled as he was jostled from side to side on top of the barrels. A pleasure drive? A miserable chore—that's what it was! Now that old Jake was gone, he had to make the trip every morning. When he got back to town, he still had to deliver the milk from house to house. That meant he had to get up an hour earlier every morning and trudge to the farm in all sorts of weather.

A pleasure drive? The first time he and Jamie had gone, the foolish dog had wagged her tail happily, as if to say, "Hi, Neil, aren't you glad we're going out together?" Stupid mutt! Ha-ha-ha! It hadn't taken him long to teach her otherwise.

Crack! Crack!

Now Jamie no longer greeted him with a wagging tail. Now he had to drag her from the doghouse. And sometimes the bitch even growled at him. But the willow switch helped. In the town, when he was calling on the customers, Neil always had to be careful. If someone saw him beating the dog, he might be bothered by the police. But here, in the dark and on the lonely country road . . . ?

"Come on, faster! You'll run, not at your speed, but at my speed. I'm in command. I'm the strongest, and I've got the switch. I'm your master!"

Crack! Crack!

Neil was sitting on a barrel in the barn. He was eating his breakfast, a can of coffee beside him. Jake had always waited to see if he'd get a second cup. But old Jake was a dupe. Neil was different. He had bothered the farmer's wife and the maid so much with his demands for more coffee every morning, that now they gave him a canful just to be rid of his begging. "Sure," thought Neil, "sit here and wait? If you want to get somewhere in this world, you have to go after it and make sure you get your share. It's always best to think of yourself first."

Jamie had sneaked into the barn too. Usually Neil made her stay outside, but this morning the door had been left ajar; very carefully and fearfully she had squeezed her body through the opening. Now she was inside where it was nice and warm, and maybe she would get something to eat. Maybe. Lately she seldom sunk her teeth into some juicy leftovers or into a bowlful of bread and bones. Jamie didn't know why she was so often neglected.

When she was forced to stay outside, she obediently lay in front of the door. Sometimes she would scratch at the latch, but it didn't help. Nobody brought her anything. When she was able to sneak inside, then Gertrude might bring her something good. But even that wasn't certain.

Everything had changed. Jamie's world had become a strange, lonely, fearsome place. She was beaten, kicked at, and scolded. At one time she had been happy and would never have thought of growling or biting, but that, too, had changed. Now she usually slunk around with her tail tucked between her legs and her mouth half open, ready to show her teeth or snap if that was necessary. She was nervous and frightened. Lashing switches, kicking boots, and a choking chain around her neck—her enemies were very powerful.

Everything had changed. And Jamie's dog brain understood but little of the human world.

A short time ago old Jake had always looked after her. Whenever the farmer's wife was very busy—which was quite often—and couldn't find the time to fix something for Jamie, old Jake would say, "Just give me a piece of bread; I'll take care of the beggar." Or little Gertrude would come with a can of milk or with some leftovers which she had gathered from the cluttered breakfast table. Then they—old Jake, Gertrude and Jamie—had celebrated in a safe corner of the barn, and they were happy: Jake and Gertrude because they were giving something, and Jamie because she was getting something.

But now it was too busy on the farm, and there was no one to help the little girl look after Jamie. Farmer Hartman never gave the dog a thought. Mrs. Hartman sometimes thought of Jamie, but she was far too busy in the morning. She would treat the dog some other time, she told herself. But that other time seldom came.

Gertrude was still not well. She wasn't allowed to go outside at all in the early morning. With the dog often left hitched to the cart, how could she take care of Jamie?

And Neil? "What's the use of feeding that dog?" he would say. "She's nothing but a nuisance, and a beggar! Old Jake has spoiled her. I leave her outside to teach her some manners. Old Jake didn't know how to train a dog!"

But this morning Jamie had sneaked inside anyway. She was famished. Neil had gotten up late and had not taken the time to feed the dog before they left. Now Jamie was sitting there, hungrily eyeing every piece of bread that went into Neil's mouth. Her eyes seemed to say, "My, that bread looks good! But why does everything go into your mouth, and nothing into mine?"

The end of her tail wagged a little, and time after time she started to jump up and move nearer. But that wicked switch was very close to Neil's hand.

Finally she took the chance. She stood up, and making a wide circle, she crept closer to Neil, coming to a halt in front of him. Cocking her head first to one side and then to the other, she begged, "Come on, give me a bite. I'm so terribly hungry."

When he saw her standing there, Neil sneered. With his large wooden shoe he kicked her in the mouth. "Get out of here!"

But suddenly a high voice sounded behind him. It trembled with anger: "Bully! You mean bully!"

Little Gertrude was standing there, her face aflame with rage and her eyes flashing with fury. Running to Jamie, she put her arms around the dog's neck and soothingly she said, "You're a good girl, Jamie. You're a good dog."

Neil sniggered. He'd show the angry child that he was the dog's master and that he could do with her whatever he wanted. "Leave that mutt alone!" he snarled.

But Gertrude stood up to him. "I won't!" she snapped back.

Just when Neil was about to drag the dog from Gertrude's arms, Mrs. Hartman entered the barn. Neil sat down again.

"Mom, does Jamie get something to eat? Come on, Mom, give her something! Please!"

"Don't get so excited, Gertrude."

"But Mom, she's so hungry! Please give her something, Mom. I'll really love you if you do." Little Gertrude tugged at Mother's apron and at her arms. She pulled Mother's head down and threw her arms around her neck; with her mouth close to Mother's ear, she begged, "Come on, Mom, she's such a poor dog, and I'll love you very much."

"But look at you!" Mother said with a start. "You're out in the barn again in your petticoat and stocking feet. You mayn't be here. It's too drafty. Get back to the kitchen!"

"But Mom, doesn't Jamie get anything?"

"Oh, all right, you little beggar. But you get back inside where it's warm. Then I'll find old flop-ears something to eat."

Gertrude dashed off. She ran down the narrow passage and opened the kitchen door.

"Come on, Jamie. Let's get going!" Neil's voice commanded from the barn door. He was tired of the child's fuss over the dog. Did they think that they could tell him what to do with that greedy mutt? He opened the door to go outside. The barrels were filled already. He only had to load them on the cart. "Come on, Jamie. Let's go!"

"No! No!" screamed little Gertrude when she heard Neil's voice. "No, Mom! No! Jamie won't get anything if she leaves now!"

"Child! Don't scream like that; you scare me. Just be quiet. I'll look after Jamie. Neil, you'll have to be patient. Just go ahead and load your cart."

Angrily Neil mumbled something about, "Who's the

dog's master, after all?" and about "spoiling the animal so she's good for nothing." But he didn't dare tell Mrs. Hartman, "Leave the dog alone. I don't want her to get anything to eat."

He heaved the barrels onto the cart, and when he returned to the barn, Jamie was feasting on leftovers of beans and bacon. The dog gulped the food down as if she expected Neil to take it away from her at any moment. Her tail was tucked between her legs in fear.

The kitchen door stood ajar, and Gertrude was peeking into the barn. She was still worried about Jamie.

"She'll make up for it; she'll pay for it on the way home!" muttered Neil.

Mrs. Hartman didn't hear him; she was busy with a cow that had her head tangled in the rope that held her to a post. Gertrude heard what Neil said. She didn't really understand what he meant, but she did know that it spelled nothing good, nothing friendly for the dog.

When the cow was settled down, Mrs. Hartman asked Neil, "How is old Jake doing?"

"Old Jake? Oh, he's been put away. You won't see him again. Well, that's no great loss."

"Put away? He's not in jail, is he? He hasn't—"

"Of course not," laughed Neil. "He got sick."

"Yes, I know that."

"Well, as far as I know they've taken him to the nursing home. I bet he never comes back. My boss is happy to be rid of the old man, and nobody else wants him."

"So, he's in the nursing home! I'm happy for him that he's taken care of. Jake was a nice, hard-working old man."

"Nobody will miss him. He has no family. But I'm extra busy now. Every morning I have to come here . . . ."

Jamie wasn't listening. She didn't understand all those words anyway. She had something good to eat. That was enough for now.

Gertrude was still at the door, and she was listening. She didn't understand all those words, but one thing she knew: Jake wasn't coming anymore. He would never come again. And suddenly a strange sadness entered her heart. Now old Jake would never help her again, and he and she and Jamie would never again sit together in that cozy corner behind the partition. And what about Jamie? Was she Neil's dog now? Did Jamie like to be Neil's dog? Oh, no! She couldn't. What a shame that Jake wouldn't come anymore, never again.

Crack! Crack!

The milk cart clattered over the road at a furious speed. The willow switch lashed down, and the breath of the racing dog came in gasps. On top of the barrels sat Neil. His eyes glittered in triumph.

Hah! Now who was the master? He was! Now he would show that his will was law!

Crack! Crack!

Behind the curtain in the kitchen window of Blue Gate Farm two eyes peered after him. They looked sad, and they looked angry too. Little Gertrude was standing

on the windowsill. When the willow switch lashed over the cart and down on the dog's back, she seemed to feel it herself.

"I love you, Jamie!" she muttered. "And I'll . . . I'll . . . ."

The cart disappeared around a bend in the road. Again the whip beat down on Jamie's back. Lurching wildly, the cart slued around the corner.

Tears burned in Gertrude's eyes. She clenched her little fist and shook it after Neil. "Bully! You mean bully!"

7. Separated

Jamie was lying in the doghouse. She was tired, and her whole body ached. Her beautiful, brown eyes were dull; sadly they looked out into the world, reflecting the silent sorrow that lived in her heart.

Whenever the door to the yard opened, she trembled with fear and cringed back into her house. Mr. Boon or little Johnny might come through the door. That would be awful. Or, worse yet, Neil might come through the door—Neil who dragged her around by the collar, who wore those hard, wooden shoes, who viciously hit her with the end of the chain that held Jamie to her house.

Old Jake had never chained her to the doghouse. While old Jake was washing the barrels or scouring the pails, he allowed Jamie to roam freely around the yard. But that was past now.

Sometimes old Jake had taken the dog with him to his one-room apartment. That had always been a treat. Then Jamie could wander about in the streets and sniff every nook and cranny she could find. But that was past now.

Sadly Jamie looked out into the world.

She didn't understand why everything had changed so much.

She was terribly thirsty. Her tongue was hot and dry. Three times she had crept out of her house as far as the chain would allow to see if there wasn't some water somewhere in a can or in an old lid. There were plenty of pails about and there was water in them too, but she couldn't reach them.

Jamie whined softly. She didn't dare bark. Barking wasn't allowed in the yard. Neil's switch and Mr. Boon's boots had told her that often enough that she wouldn't easily forget it.

But no one came to give her something to drink. So she soothed her hot tongue in the mud of a little drainage trench.

If only the gate would open and old Jake would come walking in. Why didn't he come anymore? Where had her old master gone? Didn't he know that Jamie was waiting for him and that she was thirsty? Didn't he know that the harness had chafed her chest and that those sores hurt and needed ointment? Old Jake used to do that for her. Why didn't he come now?

The gate clattered open every morning, but it was never Jake with his lantern and kind words and friendly pats on Jamie's head. Why not? Where was her old master? Jamie never saw him anymore and never caught his scent anymore. She couldn't rub her head against the wide legs of Jake's sloppy trousers anymore. She had been searching for him a long time now: in the shop, and along the streets while she was pulling the cart, and on the farm. But she hadn't found him. The chain around her neck drastically limited the area where she could sniff.

Once she had run off to seek her friendly, old master. She had raced through the store and down the streets to the alley where Jake's room was. There she had barked and whined and scratched at the door. She had put her paws on the windowsill to look inside, but she could not see anything. Jamie didn't understand that.

Old Jake had not come.

Jamie had lain down on the crumbling steps; she had put her head on her paws and waited. But old Jake hadn't come.

But Neil had.

Neil walked up with the chain in one hand and the stick in the other. Ah, now he saw that ugly mutt! When Jamie had run away, he immediately suspected that she was going to Jake's place. There lay the stupid mutt, waiting. The curtains were gone from the window and over the door hung a sign. "Room for rent," it said. The stupid mutt! But he'd teach her to run away!

"Come here, you mutt! Come here, I say!"

But it wasn't as simple as Neil thought. Jamie was at Jake's place, and Jake was her master. She was waiting for her old, faithful master, on his doorstep. What did this stranger, Neil, want from her?

Jamie growled angrily, and when Neil rattled the chain and tried to hook it to her collar, she snapped at him and jumped up so furiously that Neil stumbled back

against the windowsill of Jake's room. Yes, it wasn't going to be as easy as Neil had thought.

But Jamie never understood how sly humans are. Neil suddenly changed his approach. He went to a butcher's shop, bought a small piece of liver and gave Jamie some.

Jamie's anger died down. She got another piece, and she followed Neil. Another and another, and they were back at the store. But when she was once again chained to the doghouse, Neil gave her a beating like she had never had before.

Now Jamie didn't run away anymore.

Now Jamie knew that Neil was her master, but she couldn't understand it. She hated and she feared Neil, and in the world of dogs you must love your master.

Jamie was still waiting for Jake. But Jake didn't come. Jake never came.

Jake was lying in bed.

His tired, used-up body had finally found rest. Now, in his old age, he had finally found a spot so safe, so good that he did not wish for anything better or different. He had a bed fit for a king, and he was looked after as if he were a prince.

It had been three weeks since, sick and worn-out by hard work, he had arrived at the nursing home. "We'll put you in the bed wing until you're a little stronger," the head nurse had said. And old Jake had been tucked into a nice, clean bed with snow-white sheets, surrounded by spotless curtains.

The first days he had felt neither happy nor sad: just

sick and tired. He lay there quietly and contentedly, with his eyes closed and his arms stretched out, safe in his forgotten corner, far away from the world that had tired and worn him out.

The bed rest, the long hours and days of just lying there, had done him good. And now old Jake was growing a little stronger, he felt happy and thankful and safe. A clean bed, freshly washed clothes, tasty meals—he hadn't been so well off in years, not since his wife and his little girl had died. But that was long ago.

Yes, long, hard years had passed since old Jake had heard as many kind words as he got from the nurses now and since he had been taken care of as faithfully as he was now. His old cart had been creaking for a long time; finally it had collapsed. But now the old cart had found a good resting place. Old Jake was thankful that his heavenly Father was taking such good care of him, and that He had moved good, kind people to prepare a good home for old, worn-out toilers like him.

Here he could quietly live out his last few years. His last few years? Perhaps he would never get well again. He was already very old. Soon the Lord might call him home. That would be all right with Jake. In fact, it would be even better. It was nice in the nursing home, but heaven must be much more beautiful. Old Jake no longer feared death as he had when he was young. Old Jake knew that his Savior had died on the cross for him, and that He had prepared a place for him that was even better and safer than the best place on earth. Old Jake believed this as surely as a small boy believes his father when he promises his son something special.

But as long as he remained here on this earth, he was well taken care of. And if he did recover, if he was allowed to leave the bed wing to drink coffee and swap memories with the others, he would be as well off as a king.

He no longer had a bad-tempered boss to rush him and to tell him over and over again that he was free to leave if he didn't like it, and that an old slowpoke like him wasn't good for much anyway. He no longer had to cook his own meals, keep his shabby room clean, and sew the buttons back on his coat. He no longer had to make the trip to Blue Gate Farm every morning, rain or shine, plodding behind the cart or jarring along on top of the milk barrels.

Nevertheless, there it was again: an old pain that he couldn't forget. Yes, he was a foolish worrier. He had a pain, but it was a strange pain. It wasn't in his legs, in his head, or in his chest. The pain was in his heart.

Whenever he thought of those early mornings, or of Blue Gate Farm, he immediately thought also of Jamie. And whenever he thought of Jamie, that strange pain came back, that foolish sadness about . . . a dog!

Wasn't a dog just a dog? And hadn't he, old Jake, always treated the animal well? Now he was old and weak and could no longer take care of the animal. He could hardly ask the nursing home to take in his dog too. Besides, she wasn't even his dog. If he were wise, he would stop thinking about her.

That was just the way things were in this world: today

together, tomorrow alone. And Jamie was still strong and steady. She didn't need his pity.

Pity? No, she didn't need pity, if . . . if he were sure that she was being well-treated. But he wasn't sure of that. Oh, no, he wasn't at all sure. He knew his boss; he despised the dog. And he knew Neil too: he didn't care for animals at all; he only cared for himself.

Some people said, "Me? I wouldn't hurt my dog!" And they thought they were pretty good to their animal. But he, old Jake, would like to tap them on the shoulder and ask, "Do you ever do anything good for your dog?" What would their answer be? He believed that if you worked with an animal, you had to be good to it. That was your duty.

And now he kept worrying whenever he thought of Jamie. But wasn't it silly to worry about her? Suppose the friendly nurse asked him, "Jake, what are you brooding about? Why are you so sad?" Should he tell her about the dog, about the ugly mutt? She would laugh at him and ask him if he couldn't find anything better to worry about. She would say, "Jake, if you worried about your child, or about your grandchild, I'd understand. But this . . . ?"

But Jake no longer had a child, and he had never had a grandchild. He had no one to worry about. But he couldn't forget his dog, his good, faithful dog. He was a little ashamed of himself. He had known little old ladies who had no children to take care of and who coddled and spoiled their little dogs even more than a mother does her baby. Was he now like one of those little old ladies because he loved his dog? He had tried to forget

Jamie numerous times, but every time he began to worry anew.

But no, he wasn't like those old ladies. He loved his dog, but he had never pampered her. He was only afraid that Jamie was being abused. That was why he worried. He knew Jamie, and she didn't deserve to be mistreated. Mr. Boon and Neil really didn't know her.

In all those days and weeks he hadn't heard anything about the dog. Mr. Boon had never called at the nursing home to find out how Jake was doing and Neil hadn't been around, either. Jake didn't mind that so much, but if they had come he could have asked them about Jamie.

Jamie was unhappy, very unhappy. Jake didn't know this. He felt it.

And he, no, he could no longer do anything for her. That day was past. He could no longer wash the dust of the road from her shaggy coat. He could no longer rub soothing ointment on her chest when she had pulled a load that was too heavy for her. That day was past. He could no longer slip her part of his sandwich when the boss forgot to feed her because it was busy in the store. He could no longer take her to his room to give her leftovers from his own meal. That day was past.

Now, for better or for worse, he had to entrust her to Neil. To Neil! "Poor Jamie! Old girl! You must be very unhappy! Your old master often thinks of you, but what good does that do?"

It was a cold, clear winter night.

The bright moonlight threaded through the tall windows of the sick ward and wove a silvery sheen along the snow-white curtains around the bed. It embroidered strange, bluish silver shapes in the dark shadows.

The patients were asleep. It was very quiet.

When the steeple standing tall in the moonlit night spilled five clear notes onto the sleeping town, one of the patients awoke.

It was Jake. Of course it was Jake. His bed creaked as he hurriedly sat up. He was late! He had to get up at once, and go to the shop to pick up Jamie and the cart, and be on his way to Blue Gate Farm. He would feed the dog first so that she would have strength for the trip. Jake threw the blankets aside.

But then he saw the sick ward and the beds, and he realized that he was in that safe place with the clean sheets and curtains. An addled old man—that's what he was! He no longer had to drag his old body through the wintry night.

This happened almost every morning. Whenever the clock in the steeple struck five times, he woke up, and it always took him several minutes to remember where he was. A shiver ran down Jake's back and the old man quickly slid back into the warmth of his bed. He pulled the blankets up high. This was much better than getting up and going out into the chilly winter morning, shivering with cold. Yes, this was much better, but . . . .

In his mind Jake was riding on top of the milk barrels.

"Come on, old girl. Let's go! Giddy-up!"

Could that dog ever run! His old legs could hardly keep up. It would go better once they were across the bridge. Then he could climb on the cart. When they reached Blue Gate Farm, he would get his cup of coffee. Yes, it was a good life! Here, in the home, you didn't get a hot cup of coffee that early in the morning. The barn was always nice and warm, and when that sweet, little girl came to visit . . . .

In the cold, bright winter night, as the old man thought of days gone by, a sudden thought, a strange and beautiful thought, entered his mind. A shiver of happiness ran through him.

Forgotten was the barn and the road and the cart and the milk barrels. With his eyes closed, as if trying to lock in that beautiful thought so that it couldn't escape, Jake lay there. But his old, wrinkled face glowed with a marvelous, new joy. He had found it! He had found it!

When morning came he would carry out his beautiful plan. Would it work? Yes, yes, it might work! Suppose it did!

For a long time old Jake lay there thinking of the wonderful idea that had suddenly come into his mind. Very carefully he planned what he had to do. His old head became tired of so much thinking. If only morning would come soon!

Soft footsteps padded through the ward. It was the night nurse coming to see if her patients needed anything. Many could not help themselves.

She heard old Jake coughing and saw that he was awake. "Can't you sleep, Jake?" she asked in a whisper so she wouldn't wake the others. "Can I get you something to drink?"

Jake was a little startled; the nurse's words broke into his happy thoughts. He hardly heard what she said.

He shook his head. No, no.

But when the nurse quietly walked on, her white apron and white cap floating in the silvery moonlight as if an angel were passing by, Jake's voice rasped in sudden haste, "Nurse, nurse!"

"Yes, what is it?"

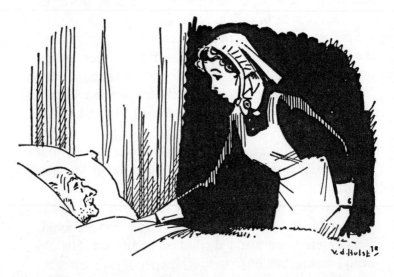

"Nurse, you see, I-I wanted . . . I wanted to ask you something . . . ."

"Of course! Aren't you comfortable?"

"Oh, yes. But, you see, I-I can't write very well; my hands tremble too much."

"Write?"

The nurse looked into the old man's happy face in surprise. What did he mean? Was he awake, or was he dreaming?

"Can you write well? Can you?"

The nurse nodded. She still didn't understand.

"You see . . . . Listen, come and sit down here, just for a minute."

Old Jake was amazed by his own boldness. He usually wasn't so bold as to ask for things. He was always afraid that they would think him a nuisance. But his beautiful new idea made him brave. Yes, sometimes in life you had to be bold. This nurse was such a kind woman.

"Tell me, Jake. What's the matter?"

She sat down on the chair beside Jake's bed and waited. The old man pushed himself up. His hands on the edge of the bed, his gray head bent toward the nurse, his eyes grave and his hoarse voice very soft—so Jake began his story.

He told the nurse of his thankfulness, and of the wonderful rest he was enjoying. He also told her of his worries about the dog.

A smile appeared on the nurse's face. The old man was worrying about a dog! She could hardly believe it. She expected him to tell her about a son, or a daughter, or about some great evil he had committed. That often happened on the sick ward. But about a dog? No, she had never before heard a story about a dog. Especially not in the middle of the night. What had gotten into old Jake!

But she listened anyway. She listened very patiently.

The moonlight fell across her back onto the bed. The

friendly light fell on his old, wrinkled hands. It put a soft sheen on his earnest face and a gloss in his thin, gray hair. Yes, she listened even though it was only to the story of a dog. She felt that the story came from the old man's heart.

The silent, surprised, almost mocking smile disappeared from her face. Jake's earnestness was so real. How could she smile about it?

When the old man, his eyes sparkling with hope, had told her his beautiful plan, she stood up. Touching his wrinkled hand for a moment, she said softly, "I'll do it. I'll write that letter, and I'll read it to you before I mail it."

Then, making hardly a sound, she continued on her rounds.

Jake sank back in the pillows. He was tired, but there was a quiet joy in his heart. It was good that he had asked the nurse right away. If you had a good plan, you should not keep it to yourself until you lost the courage to talk about it.

He closed his eyes and folded his hands.

Was he going to pray? He had always been good to Jamie, but people didn't pray for dogs, did they? And yet, Jake prayed. He prayed that the heavenly Father, who took care of all His creatures, also of the animals, would move people's hearts with compassion. That's what Jake prayed for.

For a long time the old man lay quietly.

Early in the morning a gentle hand nudged him and a voice said, "Come on, Jake; how about it? Isn't it time to wake up?" Jake was amazed to see the nurse standing beside his bed in the bright sunlight. He must have dropped off into a deep sleep. He had been dreaming about something. What was it again? It was something very beautiful. Oh, yes, he had dreamt about his little girl. She had climbed into his bed and hugged him. She was wearing a pretty, white dress and looked so sweet and happy.

But that was a long time ago . . . .

But there was also something beautiful now. What was it again? He couldn't remember. Oh, yes! Here was the nurse. She had a letter that she wanted to read to him. Oh, yes! That was it.

8. The Letter

"A letter? From whom?"

"I don't know. The handwriting is so neat; it could be from a schoolteacher."

"Let me see it."

"Here it is. Why don't you read it? Your hands are cleaner than mine." Mrs. Hartman had just been handed a letter by the mailman. Her hands were wet from kneading butter, and she was holding the clean envelope in a tip of her apron. Now she put it on the table in front of her husband.

Mr. Hartman was biting into a thick bacon sandwich, but his curiosity overcame his hunger. Quickly he wiped his greasy fingertips on his pants, rubbed his arm along his greasy chin, and tore open the letter.

"Who's it from?" Impatiently Mrs. Hartman peered over her husband's shoulder.

"Just wait a minute; I don't know yet."

"Why don't you look at the end first?"

"Oh, yes. But I don't understand it. Look, it says, 'J. Welmers, R.N.' Do you know her?"

"No, I don't. Let's read the letter."

Half aloud the farmer read the short letter while his wife listened so attentively that her lips repeated the words her husband was reading.

At the end she said, pleasantly surprised, "Oh, it's from old Jake! He can't write clearly himself, so one of the nurses has written for him."

"Yes, that's how it is. But what does the old man want from us? He asks us, you or me, to come and see him. But why? Do you understand it?"

"Well," said Mrs. Hartman jokingly, "maybe he never gets real farm butter in that home, and he wants us to bring some. Or maybe he'd like a piece of cheese or some money for tobacco. I'm sure he doesn't have a penny to his name."

"But . . . old Jake isn't a man to come begging. He never asked us for anything."

"There's always a first time. I'll pack him some butter and cheese and a piece of a sausage. And I'll put a little money with it. That'll make him happy. I don't feel like going to see him myself in that big house with all those old people. I don't know anyone there."

"Well, that's up to you. I don't have the time."

"Neither do I. Old Jake will be satisfied if we send him something."

The letter with two large grease stains on it lay half-forgotten between a piece of cheese and a rusk canister. The farmer returned to his delicious sandwich, and his wife was already looking for an old bowl or dish that she didn't want back. And the letter? And the question asked in the letter? They were already forgotten.

But suddenly there was a noise from behind the stove. Hurriedly, yet taking care not to burn herself, little Gertrude squeezed through the narrow opening. Quickly she ran after Mother and grabbed her skirt just as she was going out the door.

She had been sitting in her warm nook. That nook was her house; a footstove was her table; and a big old doll with wooden curls and painted cheeks was her child. She had been washing her child's face with the large sponge Mother used to clean the windows. She had washed it till it was dirtier and stickier than ever. Then the letter came. Suddenly she had heard Jake's name.

She hadn't understood much of the letter, nor of the

words Father and Mother had spoken, but when Father took another bite from his sandwich and Mother walked off, she became uneasy.

Mother had to go and see Jake. That was what the letter had said. That was what she had heard. Why didn't Mother do that? Jake was sick. He couldn't come here.

If only Jake could come here. Then she would tell him about Jamie. She would tell him about that nasty Neil who kicked and hit Jamie, and she would tell Jake that he had to help Jamie, that he had to come with her in the morning.

Jake didn't come anymore. Not at all. What a shame! She had told both Father and Mother about that nasty Neil. But Father had only laughed about his angry, little girl and had said that one of these days he'd go after Neil with a stick. Of course, Father was only joking. Mother had said that she couldn't boss someone else's dog.

If Jake only knew. He would help poor Jamie. If only Jake could come.

Now she ran after Mother. "Mom, Mom, are you going to see Jake? Can I come too, Mom?"

"Oh, Gertrude, you don't know what it's all about. Just go back to your doll."

"Yes, Mom, but are you going? Are you really going?"

"Go to town? Go to see old Jake? I can't very well leave my butter and all my other work and go to town as if I had nothing to do, can I? You know better than that."

"Yes, Mom. But can we go some other day? Can we, Mom? We can go together, you and I. It's not too far for me."

"Sure, sure, little nuisance, some other day. Some other day we might go. But what are we going to do there? He's an old man!"

"We can look at him, Mom. And talk to him. And we can take him some nice cookies. And there's something I want to tell him."

Suddenly Gertrude's face was very serious.

"You're a little nuisance—that's what you are!" Mother hurried out of the kitchen. Father, who had finished his sandwich and was cutting another nice slice of bacon, smiled as he called after Mother, "Now you're caught! Old Jake has found himself a good champion."

Gertrude climbed on Father's knee. "Are you coming too?"

"Me? What an idea!"

"Will you come, Daddy?"

"Nothing doing! You can go with Mother. Tuesday it's market day in town, and your mother will be going out then."

"Tuesday it's market. Tuesday! Tuesday!" She'd remember that. That was in one, two . . . , four days. Tuesday!

On Tuesday Mrs. Hartman, all dressed up, went to town. She carried a large shopping basket, and Gertrude skipped along beside her. She was warmly dressed in a heavy coat, and a woolen hat and scarf to keep out the cold. She linked her arm in Mother's.

Mother looked a little uneasy. In her basket were some

butter, cheese, and a piece of smoked meat. She would drop that off at the nursing home for Jake. But she would not go inside where all those strange, old people were. No, that she wouldn't do.

"Mom, are dogs allowed to live where Jake is living? Old dogs?"

"Dogs? Well, Gertrude—"

"Mom, is old Jake always going to stay there? Can't he ever go home again? And who's the boss of the nurs'ry home? Is he a nice man, Mom?"

"Well, Gertrude—"

"Oh, Mom, I'm so happy we're going to see old Jake. Are you too, Mom?"

"See old Jake? Who says we're going to see him?"

"Ha-ha-ha!" laughed Mr. Hartman, closing the farm gate behind them. "Ha-ha-ha! You're caught, Mother!"

When his wife angrily looked back at him, he called after her, "It's all right. Say hello to the old man for me!"

It was a week later, early in the morning.

A steady drizzle was falling and drops of water slowly wound their way down the glistening trunks of the trees. The rain glittered on the thatched roof of Blue Gate Farm in thousands of milky pearls and soaked into the farm's driveway. It was a murky, chilly day. Amid the bare, wet trees, the farm looked sad and forlorn in the gray world.

Harnessed between the two long shafts of the milk

cart, Jamie lay on the muddy driveway waiting for Neil. Neil had gone into the warm barn. He no longer untied the dog when they arrived at Blue Gate Farm in the morning. It was too much trouble for him. Whenever he let her loose, he always had trouble with the little girl who wanted to feed the dog. Besides, each time he had to put the dog back into the harness again. So he just let her lie outside. That was easier. And what did it matter? She was only a dog.

Jamie lay in the mud. Her tired body, steaming from the fast run to the farm, heaved up and down as she panted. Her shaggy head rested on her large paws as she stared sadly out into the world with her big, brown eyes. Her thick, dirty tail drooped in the mud.

The rain drizzled down steadily and clung to Jamie's glistening coat. A thin stream of water trickled between her ears into one of her eyes. She shook her head, and lay still again until another trickle came down to tease her.

Around the corner the latch of the barn door rattled.

With a start, Jamie tried to stand up, but she couldn't do it very fast: her legs and back were too stiff and sore. But if it was her master coming, she had to be careful! He would yank her up by the head or kick her if she didn't get up quickly enough. Jamie trembled for her master, and her eyes looked fearfully in the direction from which he'd come.

But the wooden shoes that came wading through the mud were small ones. It was little Gertrude who came running around the corner toward Jamie.

Ah! Jamie straightened up and the raindrops flew off

her wagging tail. Her whole body squirmed with joy; her forepaws pranced up and down; and the milk cart danced up and down too. Jamie stretched her neck and greeted Gertrude with a happy howl. When Gertrude came, her little friend, the only one who was kind to her, all at once Jamie was the old, spirited, happy dog she used to be—the exuberant cart dog with the friendly, brown eyes and the joyful bark.

The little girl grabbed Jamie's head. Ugh! It was wet! But she didn't let go. She took the dog's long ears and rubbed them over her brown eyes. She danced with glee and cried, "Listen, Jamie! Listen! You know what, Jamie?"

She squatted down beside Jamie and pulled her big head down beside hers.

Whenever little Gertrude was happy, Jamie became happy too—happy and playful. Her wet tongue found Gertrude's nose, and she wanted to dance around the girl just like she used to do. But the cart held her back. She lunged and squirmed . . . . One shaft bumped Gertrude's shoulder and knocked her down. Ugh! There she sat on the wet ground, her hands in the mud.

"Calm down, you naughty dog!" she grumbled. "I was just going to tell you something very nice." She scrambled up again, wiped her muddy hands on Jamie's glistening back, and forgot about the mishap. She thought only of the exciting news she had to tell the dog.

Quickly now, afraid that she would start jumping about again, Gertrude told Jamie that Father had gone to town to the market. And her eyes sparkled with joy as she added that he would go to Mr. Boon too, and that . . . .

But Jamie didn't understand the wonderful story at all. Jamie had no taste for words. Jamie liked bones and leftovers. Hungrily she sniffed Gertrude's hands and pushed her nose under the girl's apron to find out whether she was hiding something there.

"Sit still, you silly dog!" she scolded. "Sit still and listen!"

This morning Jamie shouldn't care about bones and leftovers. The wonderful news that Gertrude had to tell her was much better than the best food! No, today Jamie would get nothing. With Father gone to market, Mother was far too busy. And Neil, that nasty Neil, didn't want to help her at all. Jamie would have to go hungry one more time, but tomorrow . . . ! Tomorrow!

She stroked Jamie's head and again started telling her about Father who was going to see Mr. Boon, Jamie's owner. And Father had lots of money in his wallet.

But the beautiful story made Jamie impatient. If she wasn't getting anything to eat, she wanted to play with her friend. She wanted to play a wild game; she wanted to jump and romp just like they used to when the world was still good and happy. Jamie forgot all about the harness that held her to the cart. She jumped up and put both huge paws on Gertrude's shoulders. The poor child almost buckled under the sudden heavy load, and she cried, "Oh, Jamie! Jamie! Let go! Down!" She twisted away from under the dog's dirty paws and ran off. With a wild, exuberant lunge, Jamie went after her.

Oh no! The swaying milk cart banged into a tree, and the dog was jerked back so violently that her paws slipped in the slick mud and she was knocked down. All at once Jamie's playfulness was gone. She struggled up again under the heavy shafts and looked back at the awkward cart in fear. Was that cart also an angry master who wouldn't allow her even a little bit of fun?

Little Gertrude stopped at the corner of the barn, up-set when she saw Jamie fall. Poor Jamie! It was the dog's own fault, but she felt sorry for her. Wait, she would try to find something for her to eat after all. But when she walked to the door, she bumped into Neil, who was just coming from the barn with a heavy barrel of milk on his shoulders.

"Keep out of my way!" he snapped. And when he saw that the milk cart had hit a tree beside the driveway and that the dog was covered with mud, he became furious. He cursed angrily.

Putting the barrel of milk down, he walked up to Jamie, his face mottled with rage.

"What did you do, you stupid mutt!"

Jamie cringed. She tucked her tail between her legs and coiled her head under one of the shafts of the cart.

"Take that! And that!" She got a couple of mean kicks, and Neil grabbed her by the neck and dragged her to the entrance of the barn to load the barrels.

Jamie wanted to walk; she was even willing to run if she had to. But she was too frightened, and in her fright she cringed, and trembled, and groveled along the ground. Her paws with their dull, outspread nails dug into the mud as she drew back in fear from Neil's hands.

This made Neil even more furious. Wait! He'd cure that stubborn loafer of her tricks. He'd give her such a hard and thorough lesson that she'd never even think of doing something she wasn't supposed to. Yonder lay a piece of wood.

Neil got it and swung it high.

But then little Gertrude came flying at him. "No! No, you bully! You can't do that!" she screamed. She was so angry she was crying. She clutched at his leg with both hands tugging and twisting to stop the angry hothead.

"Get away, you little pest!"

"No, I won't! I won't!"

He pushed her aside, but she grabbed his jacket with one hand and his pantleg with the other and, screaming, she let herself be dragged along. Neil flung the piece of wood down. He was afraid of those screams. If Mrs. Hartman heard them . . . . He wanted to remain on her good side. She was a soft touch. When you put on a woebegone face and fed her a line about being hungry or having a weak stomach, she usually was good for a piece of cheese or ham, or a couple of fresh eggs, or sometimes even a little change.

He wrested himself free from Gertrude and started to load the barrels, scolding all the while.

Gertrude ran into the barn. She was very angry with Neil, but she was also very shocked by what she had done in her anger. She was fighting off a crying spell. She looked for Mother. She wanted to bury her head in Mother's skirt and sob out her anger and compassion. But Mother wasn't in the barn, and she wasn't in the kitchen either.

So little Gertrude hurriedly climbed on the window-sill and knelt there to watch Jamie run down the driveway, out the gate and down the road.

The rain kept flinging tiny water globules against the glass. She could hardly see outside. But she lifted the curtain aside, pushed her nose against the cold pane, and waited. Her great happiness was gone. Suppose what Mother had said this morning was true? What if Jamie's owner, Mr. Boon, told Father he didn't want to sell the dog?

Crack! Crack!

There was Jamie now. Her paws clawed the mud as she picked up speed. She was terribly dirty! She was covered with mud.

Little Gertrude trembled and pulled her head back.

Crack! Crack!

But she had to look again.

No, she didn't want to think of what Mother had said. She only wanted to think of the beautiful thing that would happen tomorrow.

"Poor Jamie! Don't be afraid!"

Her eyes filled with both compassion and happiness as she stared after the milk cart through the glistening raindrops. Under her breath she whispered, "Don't be afraid, Jamie. Don't pay any mind if that nasty Neil beats you. Just run. Run as fast as you can. Father is going to buy you from Mr. Boon. Old Jake has asked Mother to do that, and Mr. Boon can't say no. Neil won't be your master anymore, and you'll live with us. In the morning, in the afternoon, at night—you'll always be here. You'll be our watchdog. You'll get a nice house, and lots of bones. And we'll play together. I'll even put a nice ribbon around your neck. Don't pay any mind if that bully scolds you: tomorrow . . . ."

In her happiness little Gertrude bounced up and down on her knees.

"Oh, tomorrow! I know it, and you know it too, don't you Jamie? I told you when we were together. But Neil, that mean bully, doesn't know anything about it. Only we know it—you and I."

The milk cart disappeared around the bend.

9. The Visit

After the long winter, spring had finally come.

One beautiful morning, as the bright sunshine poured down on the happy world, and the birds were singing among the blossoming trees in the orchard, an old man walked along a lonely country road. Slowly, step by step, he strolled on. He walked like someone who had lots of time, and who loved to have the sun shining on his back and hear the birds singing merrily and see the flowers beaming up at the sky.

It was old Jake.

Jake could walk faster, but he didn't. Why should he? He had plenty of time. He had told the nurse he was going to stay out all day long, and Blue Gate Farm wasn't very far away.

Throughout the winter he had been sickly and weak, but two weeks ago he had gone outside for the first time this spring. It had done him a lot of good, and since then he had grown stronger and stronger.

It wasn't good for him to be inside so much. The fresh air, the sun and the wind, the rain and the cold—they were much better, much healthier for him. When he went to Blue Gate Farm every morning and delivered the milk around town, or washed the barrels and scoured the pails in the drafty courtyard, he got plenty of fresh air.

But that seemed a long, long time ago. Now he couldn't do it anymore. His knees were too weak and his hands trembled too much. No, it was a good thing that he could walk at his leisure, dressed like a gentleman.

From an orchard bursting with apple blossoms two playful finches dove down to the road. They hopped about twittering merrily. Old Jake stopped and watched the birds for a moment. Their feathers blazed with colors in the sunshine. The sight of them quickened Jake's heart with gladness. The beauty of the day made the old man feel young again.

As he walked on, a warm thankfulness flooded his heart like the bright sun flooded the world around him with its warmth. He felt extremely well-off in his old age. Old Jake strolled between the cheering fields like an old king viewing his kingdom.

But he was even richer than a king. A king still had cares and worries, but Jake had no more worries. His heavenly Father had made his life beautiful and peaceful. This happy day was also a gift from Him. Jake looked up at the sunny sky as if sending his thankfulness upward in a silent prayer.

Yes, it was a beautiful, happy day. It was the first time he dared to go for such a long walk, but he was doing fine and he was well on his way. They would be surprised to see him coming at Blue Gate Farm. Ahead were the small roadside bungalows already. Soon he would see the old, hollow willow tree which Jamie could never pass without barking at it. At one time a swarm of wasps had lived in the tree and one warm summer day two of them had stung Jamie on the nose. She never forgot that.

Jamie . . . . The thought of her made Jake's happy day even happier. Today he'd see his faithful dog again. A long time had passed since he had seen her. Would she still know him? Of course! A dog never forgot its master!

Jake thrust his hand deep into his coat pocket. He knew that Jamie had everything she could want, but he still had something for her in his pocket: a few pennies worth of liver from the butcher. And a nice chocolate bar for the sweet, little girl. She certainly deserved it. If it hadn't been for little Gertrude, Jamie's life would have been very grim indeed.

Again he thought back to that morning in the sick ward when Mrs. Hartman and little Gertrude had come. No, at first Mrs. Hartman hadn't been at all interested in buying that ugly mutt for a farm dog. But then the little girl's face had grown very sad. At first, when she had heard what Jake was asking her mother, she had danced with pleasure. "Yes, Mom! Let's buy Jamie! Yes!" She had jumped up and down on the wooden floor and made such a racket that the nurse had warned, "Shhh! Not so much noise, little girl!"

When her mother had refused, the girl's face had grown so sad that even Jake had felt sorry for her. Sobbing, she had hidden her face in her mother's skirt. And finally Mrs. Hartman had given in. At heart she was a good woman; maybe a little fickle and moody, but good nevertheless.

But it was the girl who had saved Jamie.

"Yes, yes, old girl," mumbled Jake, "you don't understand any of it, and you don't know what happened, but little Gertrude saved you."

Bravely the old man walked on. He yearned to see the dog, and the girl, and the quiet corner in the barn, the corner that belonged to them.

Mr. Hartman was sitting at the table. He was counting his money. His wife was down on her knees sweeping under the table. Gertrude was trying to curl dandelion stems in a cup of water.

Suddenly they all looked up with a start. What was that? What was the matter with Jamie? Just a minute ago she was quietly basking in the sun, and now, all at once, she was carrying on as if a whole gang of thieves were sneaking onto the yard.

"Listen to that!" said Mrs. Hartman, peering out from under the table.

"Yes, I wonder what's gotten into that dog?"

Jamie was chained to the doghouse, and they heard her jerking at the chain and digging her paws in the gravel. She barked furiously and impatiently; she howled and whined. The doghouse banged up and down as Jamie strained at the chain.

Mr. Hartman jumped up and craned his neck to look out the window so he could see the dog and find out what was going on. His wife, still on her knees, crawled

forward and pulled herself up by his shirt. Little Gertrude squeezed herself between Father and the window.
She wanted to see too. She bumped her head on the
windowsill, but she hardly noticed. What was the matter with Jamie?

And suddenly there she was, lunging past the window,
her tongue hanging from her panting mouth and her
chain almost choking her. Thumping along behind her
came the heavy doghouse. She was headed toward the
gate. They stared in amazement and wonder.

But . . . who was that? At the gate stood an old gentleman.

"Who's that, Mom?"

"I don't know. Look, he's coming in. Is that why
the dog is making all that noise? Look, she is trying to
get at him! Oh, she's going to hurt the man! She's going
to tear the old man to pieces!

"Jamie! Jamie!" Mrs. Hartman shouted through the window in fear. "Jamie, you bad dog, come back!"

"What in the world!" the farmer exclaimed angrily. "I've never seen her acting like that."

"Oh, Mom! Look at her, Mom!"

Fiercely, the dog leaped at the old man, barking and howling. She fell back, she squirmed and wriggled crazily, and then leaped at the man again. She had her paws on his shoulders, and was pushing her wet nose in his face.

"Go and help the poor old fellow!" Mother called nervously to her husband.

"Yes, but . . . I can't understand it. Is that dog angry, or is she—"

"Never mind! Just help that man. Oh, look!"

The old man staggered and dropped his cane. But he didn't look at all frightened by the attack. He grabbed the dog by the head and rumpled it between his hands.

But the dog squirmed out of his grip and leaped again.

Oh, no! The old man stumbled back against the gatepost, and his beautiful new hat rolled across the road.

"Oh, look! It's Jake!" cried Mrs. Hartman when she saw the friendly face and the white hair, which had been hidden by the hat. "Well, have you ever!"

"Jake! Jake!" shouted Gertrude, and she raced out of the kitchen through the barn and into the yard.

"Well, well! I didn't recognize him all dressed up," laughed the farmer. "Now I understand that crazy dog."

Mother followed Gertrude. Mr. Hartman tapped on the window and wagged his head admiringly as if to say, "My, my, Jake, do you ever look the gentleman!"

But Jake didn't see him. He was much too busy with his old friend, who was giving him such a wild, exuberant welcome.

"Calm down, old girl! Yes, you're a good dog. Quiet now! Let your old master . . . . Shhh! Behave yourself. Yes, your old master is with you again. My hat, my hat!"

Old Jake hobbled after his black hat and stooped to pick it up. But Jamie, still dragging the doghouse, leaped at him again and almost knocked him head over heels. Suddenly Jamie calmed down. She smelled something delicious, but where was it? It was somewhere in Jake's clothes, but where? She sniffed and snorted greedily and tried to stick her nose into the pocket of Jake's coat.

"Well! Such bad manners!" grumbled Jake in a feigned anger. "Has your old master lost all control over you? That's not the way. Come here!" He had hold of his hat now and hastily slapped it back on his head. Seizing Jamie by the neck, he said, "Here girl, let me untie you. Look what you've done to your house, you rascal! Come along to the house!"

Now Gertrude came running around the corner. Mother was right behind her, beaming with pleasure at the sight of the old man. She laughed and called to him, "Will you look at yourself! You must be having a rough life!"

Jake came staggering up the driveway. His hat was

perched crookedly on his mussed white hair and his face was flushed with excitement. His new brown coat was soiled by Jamie's paws and his cane dangled from his coat pocket. He was having difficulty hanging on to the panting, snorting, lunging dog. "Yes, yes," he panted, "if only that dog would calm down."

"Jake! Jake!" cried Gertrude.

"Hello, Jake. Did you decide to take the day off and pay us a visit?" asked Mrs. Hartman. "That's nice of you, really nice. But look at your clothes! Just let that dog go!"

"Yes, but if I let go of her she'll—" panted Jake.

"Jim, we need your help!" Mother called to the farm-hand who had also come out to see what the noise was all about. "Put that wild dog back in the doghouse."

"The doghouse? But where is it?"

"There!" said Mother, pointing. "Jamie thought she had a mobile home."

"Come inside, Jake, and rest a while. You look as if you've been in a fight. My, you've got a nice hat! Come on in!"

"Yes, yes," panted Jake. "That dog did not forget me. But she's so wild!" They filed into the barn: first Mother, then Jake, and little Gertrude dancing around them. Mr. Hartman was waiting at the kitchen door. "Come in, come in! Man, we never expected such important company today."

"Hello, Mr. Hartman. My, that dog—"

"Here, sit down and rest. That dog must have tired

you out. No, don't sit there. Take the easy chair; it's more comfortable. Man, your new hat looks a mess. My wife will brush it off for you. How are you, Jake? Are you all better again?"

Jake didn't answer. He sat down on the chair and wearily closed his eyes. His hands were trembling and his cheeks were pale. Sharp creases showed around his mouth. He was exhausted.

Mrs. Hartman shook her head at her husband as if to say, "Let him be for a minute; he's all in."

But Jake soon recovered. He was a little ashamed of himself that he had been unable to answer. These good people were so kind to him. Come, he should perk up a little. He straightened up.

"Come here a minute, little girl," he said to Gertrude. His voice was filled with warmth and his eyes with thankfulness. Gertrude thought that Jake wanted to shake her hand, but he pushed her hand into the pocket of his coat. "Here," he said, "I brought you something."

With a happy face Gertrude dug into the pocket. She heard something crackling, and a crumpled little package came out of the pocket. She looked at it wonderingly. What was in it? It was probably something to eat. It was soft. She unwrapped it.

Jake wasn't looking at her. He was busy talking to the farmer. But when Gertrude opened the paper, her face darkened and she turned up her nose. Ugh! They were wet, slippery, brown things. Ugh!

Mother saw Gertrude's upturned nose and her disappointed face, and suddenly she laughed aloud. "Ha-ha-ha! Look at the way Jake treats the child!"

Surprised, Jake looked at the paper in Gertrude's hands. "Oh, my dear girl. I'm sorry. That's not for you. That's for Jamie. I put your hand in the wrong pocket. Here, I'll take that back. Look at what I have here."

Gertrude got her chocolate bar.

"That's for you. That's because you . . . because you," old Jake pushed the bar into Gertrude's warm hand as if he wanted to put all his joy and gratitude into that hand too, "because you've been so good to my dog. That's why!"

Jake had a wonderful day.

He was served coffee and cake, and it tasted better than anything he had ever had at Blue Gate Farm before. He had dinner at the farm, and Mrs. Hartman treated him like a starving young fellow who hadn't had anything to eat for days. She kept filling his plate. And he smoked three of Mr. Hartman's cigars.

But it wasn't the good food that made the day so wonderful. It was the thankful joy in his heart that made him happy. He was flooded by happy thoughts as he strolled around the farm in the beautiful spring weather. Little Gertrude and Jamie kept him company.

The farmer and his wife were much too busy to spend all their time with Jake, and the old man didn't mind. It was nice enough of them to receive him so kindly. They treated him as if he were a relative, and he was only the man that used to come to pick up the milk. Jamie had a nice home here. She was just as well off here as he was in the nursing home.

"Yes, old girl, we're all set, you and I." Jake could easily see that the dog was well cared for, just like all the other animals on the farm.

In their old corner in the barn, behind the partition, Jamie ate the liver and a few pieces of bread. She wasn't as hungry as she used to be. She also showed Gertrude all the tricks Jake had taught her through the years.

They walked and they talked and they played.

In the warm afternoon, when Jake was sitting on a bench in the sunshine, leaning against the barn, he dozed off. His hat slipped down over his nose. Loyal Jamie lay at his feet as if she was guarding her old master. As he sat there dozing, Gertrude filled his pockets with hay. She had seen him pick up some long blades of hay to take home. He would use them as pipe cleaners. Gertrude wanted to make sure that he had plenty.

Yes, Jake had a wonderful day.

But when the golden sun began to set, when it grew bigger and bigger until it was a red ball of fire in the distant sky of the waning day, it was time for Jake to go.

As he got ready to leave, he thanked them all. He thanked them at least five times for the wonderful day. And once again—it must be for the fifth time too—he told them how glad he was that Jamie had found a good home.

Mr. and Mrs. Hartman and Gertrude walked him to the gate. They stopped at the doghouse where Jamie was chained once more. Usually she was free to roam around the farm, but because Jake was leaving, the farmer had chained her, so she wouldn't follow her old master.

"Goodbye, old girl. I'm on my way again."

Jamie received a few loving pats on the head. She didn't understand what was going on, but she became very nervous. She danced up and down, jerked at her chain, and barked impatiently.

"No, girl, you can't come along. It's impossible. Your master is going back to the home, and there's no place for dogs there. Quiet! Calm down! Here you're well cared for as I am over there. So just be quiet now! No, you can't come with me."

Hurriedly old Jake walked on. Once he was around the bend and the dog could no longer see him, she would calm down.

"Goodbye, Mr. and Mrs. Hartman. Goodbye, Gertrude. Yes, I'll be back again, the Lord willing. And a good night to all of you."

"Bye, Jake. Have a nice walk."

"Bye, Jake!"

"Bye, sweetheart. You're a splendid girl."

Jamie barked furiously. She wanted to go with Jake. How could she stay when her master was going? She howled and whined; she jerked and pulled at the chain, but Jim had nailed the doghouse to a post in the ground to make sure that she never dragged it away again.

Woof! Woof!

Jake walked as fast as his legs would carry him. He didn't even look back. "The poor animal! She doesn't understand how well-off she is. She wants to come with me."

Soon he was at the bend in the road.

The golden evening sun threw a strange, beautiful

light on the blooming orchards. It made them glow like rich, golden satin. In the silence of the falling evening a distant bird sang a late song. The road was very quiet.

The violet light on the far horizon reflected in Jake's old, tired eyes. To him it seemed like a silent promise of a world much more beautiful than this one—a new world of perfect happiness.

The old man stood still and bared his head.

"Lord God, I thank You. I'm so happy. But my heart, oh Lord God, my heart yearns for You and for Your glory!"

As Jake made his way back to town, his heart brimming with gratitude, his two best friends were sitting together in front of the doghouse.

For a long time Jamie had whined and howled. At last Mr. Hartman chased her into the doghouse: "That's enough, you noisy mutt!" When she kept on whining, Jim took the broom and banged it on the roof of the doghouse. It frightened Jamie, and her sadness grew even greater. Old, bad memories came to her mind.

Jamie didn't understand the strange world of people.

First there was nothing but happiness; then sorrow came back. This morning suddenly her old, almost forgotten master had returned. But now he had left again. Why?

Jamie lifted her head and peered down the lonely, empty road. She whined softly. Softly she called for her old master to come back.

Then Gertrude came. She knelt down and put her arm

around the dog's neck. "Don't cry, Jamie," she said. She talked about all kinds of good things: about soup bones and bacon rinds, about games in the empty hayloft, about a new collar she'd buy at the market, and about old Jake who would come back sometime.

Jamie didn't understand much of it. Human words didn't mean much to her, but she did understand what human eyes told her.

She fixed her trusting, brown eyes on little Gertrude, and her tail began to wag. Suddenly her long tongue came out and found Gertrude's chin.

That meant, "As long as you stay with me, I'll be happy too."

Books by W.G. Vandehulst

Stories Children Love Series:

1. *The Little Wooden Shoe*
2. *Through the Thunderstorm*
3. *Bruno the Bear*
4. *The Basket*
5. *Lost in the Snow*
6. *Annie and the Goat*
7. *The Black Kitten*
8. *The Woods beyond the Wall*
9. *My Master and I*
10. *The Pig under the Pew*
11. *Three Little Hunters*
12. *The Search for Christmas*
13. *Footprints in the Snow*

Other Titles:

1. *The Mystery of Old Abe*
2. *Pierre and His Friends*
3. *The Night before Christmas*
4. *The Little Girl and the Big Bell*
5. *The Old Man and His Dog*
6. *The Window in the Roof*
7. *My Favorite Story Book*